NoFood

Conversation Pieces

A Small Paperback Series from Aqueduct Press
Subscriptions available: www.aqueductpress.com

1. The Grand Conversation
    Essays by L. Timmel Duchamp

2. With Her Body
    Short Fiction by Nicola Griffith

3. Changeling
    A Novella by Nancy Jane Moore

4. Counting on Wildflowers
    An Entanglement by Kim Antieau

5. The Traveling Tide
    Short Fiction by Rosaleen Love

6. The Adventures of the Faithful Counselor
    A Narrative Poem by Anne Sheldon

7. Ordinary People
    A Collection by Eleanor Arnason

8. Writing the Other
    A Practical Approach
    by Nisi Shawl & Cynthia Ward

9. Alien Bootlegger
    A Novella by Rebecca Ore

10. The Red Rose Rages (Bleeding)
    A Short Novel by L. Timmel Duchamp

11. Talking Back: Epistolary Fantasies
    edited by L. Timmel Duchamp

12. Absolute Uncertainty
    Short Fiction by Lucy Sussex

13. Candle in a Bottle
    A Novella by Carolyn Ives Gilman

14. Knots
    Short Fiction by Wendy Walker

15. Naomi Mitchison: A Profile of Her Life and Work
    A Monograph by Lesley A. Hall

16. We, Robots
    A Novella by Sue Lange

17. Making Love in Madrid
    A Novella by Kimberly Todd Wade

18. Of Love and Other Monsters
    A Novella by Vandana Singh

19. Aliens of the Heart
    Short Fiction by Carolyn Ives Gilman

20. Voices From Fairyland:
    The Fantastical Poems of Mary Coleridge, Charlotte
    Mew, and Sylvia Townsend Warner
    Edited and With Poems by Theodora Goss

21. My Death
    A Novella by Lisa Tuttle

22. De Secretis Mulierum
    A Novella by L. Timmel Duchamp

23. Distances
    A Novella by Vandana Singh

24. Three Observations and a Dialogue:
    Round and About SF
    Essays by Sylvia Kelso and a correspondence
    with Lois McMaster Bujold

25. The Buonarotti Quartet
    Short Fiction by Gwyneth Jones

26. Slightly Behind and to the Left
    Four Stories & Three Drabbles by Claire Light

27. Through the Drowsy Dark
    Short Fiction and Poetry
    by Rachel Swirsky

28. Shotgun Lullabies
    Stories and Poems by Sheree Renée Thomas

29. A Brood of Foxes
    A Novella by Kristin Livdahl

30. The Bone Spindle
    Poems and Short Fiction by Anne Sheldon

31. The Last Letter
    A Novella by Fiona Lehn

32. We Wuz Pushed
    On Joanna Russ and Radical Truth-Telling
    by Brit Mandelo

33. The Receptionist and Other Tales
    Poems by Lesley Wheeler

34. Birds and Birthdays
    Stories by Christopher Barzak

35. The Queen, the Cambion, and Seven Others
    Stories by Richard Bowes

36. Spring in Geneva
    A Novella by Sylvia Kelso

37. The XY Conspiracy
    A Novella by Lori Selke

38. Numa
    An Epic Poem
    by Katrinka Moore

39. Myths, Metaphors, and Science Fiction:
    Ancient Roots of the Literature of the Future
    Essays by Sheila Finch

40. NoFood
    Short Fiction by Sarah Tolmie

41. The Haunted Girl
    Poetry and Short Stories by Lisa M. Bradley

About the Aqueduct Press Conversation Pieces Series

The feminist engaged with sf is passionately interested in challenging the way things are, passionately determined to understand how everything works. It is my constant sense of our feminist-sf present as a grand conversation that enables me to trace its existence into the past and from there see its trajectory extending into our future. A genealogy for feminist sf would not constitute a chart depicting direct lineages but would offer us an ever-shifting, fluid mosaic, the individual tiles of which we will probably only ever partially access. What could be more in the spirit of feminist sf than to conceptualize a genealogy that explicitly manifests our own communities across not only space but also time?

Aqueduct's small paperback series, Conversation Pieces, aims to both document and facilitate the "grand conversation." The Conversation Pieces series presents a wide variety of texts, including short fiction (which may not always be sf and may not necessarily even be feminist), essays, speeches, manifestoes, poetry, interviews, correspondence, and group discussions. Many of the texts are reprinted material, but some are new. The grand conversation reaches at least as far back as Mary Shelley and extends, in our speculations and visions, into the continually-created future. In Jonathan Goldberg's words, "To look forward to the history that will be, one must look at and retell the history that has been told." And that is what Conversation Pieces is all about.

L. Timmel Duchamp

Jonathan Goldberg, "The History That Will Be" in Louise Fradenburg and Carla Freccero, eds., *Premodern Sexualities* (New York and London: Routledge, 1996)

Published by Aqueduct Press
PO Box 95787
Seattle, WA 98145-2787
www.aqueductpress.com

ISBN: 978-1-61976-065-3

Cover illustration: Copyright © Can Stock Photo Inc./kosta57
www.canstockphoto.com

Original Block Print of Mary Shelley by Justin Kempton:
www.writersmugs.com

Printed in the USA by Applied Digital Imaging

Conversation Pieces
Volume 40

NoFood

by
Sarah Tolmie

"We meten so selden, by stok other stone"

— *Pearl*

Contents

NoFood...1

The Last Supper...10

Gringo 19

Cakes and Ale...30

Crystalline Donuts..53

Cena 69

NoFood

Her parents had gotten her a reservation at the restaurant for her eighteenth birthday. There is no need to ask which restaurant. They had put her name on the waiting list when she was sixteen, plus two guests—anonymous guests, for whose friends are the same at eighteen as at sixteen? They were not sanguine about their chances of being invited themselves—too old, too ugly. What made it utterly out of the question, finally, was the fact that neither of them had had the procedure by that time. Seychelles had been among the first clients once the process was indemnified; hers was the TGB generation. It was going to save them millions in surgery later: parents with any sense looked upon it as a cost-saving measure. So on the evening of her eighteenth birthday, her proud parents saw her into the security helicopter, with her wrist corsage and her two most beautiful friends, Rihoku and Donovan, TGBers, too, and retired to have dinner with their personal trainers behind the reinforced windows of their apartment block. "Thank God they have one-way glass," Seychelles said, "or everyone would see them eating. Right on the main street. It's disgusting." Her friends giggled in their safety straps.

They arrived on the helipad at precisely 7:02 and were photographed by the blogbots of the main papers, looking gorgeously windswept in the dwindling chop of the overhead blades. All the bots were anchored to the roof because of the constant storm of copter blades they had to endure; every now and again the bolts loosened and one would scud off to drop like a bomb for two hundred floors. They were programmed to erase after 15 feet of free fall, so nobody worried about them. Seychelles, Hoku, and Donovan, having talked it over in the helicopter, faced the cameras—or did not quite face them—in animated but serious conversation, in which they contrived to look intelligent, engaging, busy, and to show their teeth at the same time.

They proceeded coolly inside past the checkpoint and were seated at their table, a small round frame of Lucite with mahogany beach chairs. Each of the tables in the restaurant was filled with water, a few waving fronds, and neutral-colored pebbles; and each guest was served on a floating tray of balsa wood. "Both woods just off the watch list," said Donovan admiringly as she sat down. She was doing embargo law; her father was the city's foremost nenvironmentalist. He could get around anything. They looked down into the reflective surface of their table. It was rare to see so much water at once. After they had peered down at it for some time, they noticed tiny translucent fish flickering past. "Gross," said Hoku, "they must shit in there."

"Exactly," said the busboy, appearing at his elbow in a raffia apron. It looked like he had lost a battle with a ball of furry twine. "Some patrons were actually drinking the water."

"Gross," said Hoku again.

"Yes," said the busboy, "and quite against our philosophy. If they want to drink, they can drink at home."

"Quite so," said Donovan, looking affronted. Seychelles smiled at the correctness of their sentiments. That was why she had brought them. She had known they would fit in.

"Would you like to see the wine list?" asked the busboy.

"Of course not," replied Seychelles. "Even thinking about alcohol is a waste of time. Please bring us the appetizer menu." The busboy looked at her appraisingly. Seychelles refused to care about impressing a busboy. Some things were obvious. As her mother always said: those who can't afford doctors self-medicate. "Thank you." The busboy departed in a twirl of raffia.

The waiter who returned with their menus was ten years older, as they instantly understood by the fact that he appeared ten years younger. He wore no raffia and instead of alertness exerted an air of command. He set their calligraphic menus lightly and precisely on their balsa wood trays, causing scarcely a ripple. "Pure cotton paper," he said, "hand-ground ink, reed pen."

"Thank you," said Seychelles graciously. He made some subtle hand gesture without moving that powerfully suggested a bow and moved away.

"What's a reed?" whispered Hoku apologetically.

"Kind of grass. Grows in water," replied Donovan, trying to pick up her menu without getting it wet. Seychelles grabbed hers without fuss and looked it over. Nothing too unexpected. The fashion for complexity was over. Almost everything from the Asias was tainted now, no use even buying it contraband. She saw the word *mangosteen*. Engineered, maybe. It seemed improper. Perhaps they could be grown in hothouses. She would ask about it. The point was that they were supposed to be able to make anything you ordered. What else were you paying for?

They mulled things over in silence. Seychelles wondered about her friends' strategies. Had they been practicing for weeks, pulling out their grandmothers' vintage cookbooks? She had read over a few of those herself. One ancient e-vol, compatible with hardly anything her parents had, had been called *The Joy of Cooking*. Now there was a word she had never heard anyone use. *Joy*. It sounded religious, made her think of fundos. There had been a recipe for squirrel. There were still squirrels; she had seen a few on campus. Of course, maybe there were only squirrels in places with armed guards. She had also read restaurant reviews going back twenty years or so. Some of these were surprising: it had never occurred to her that people would travel all over the world to go to certain restaurants. None of her friends traveled, for reasons too boring to think about: risk, disease, security ennui. That people once flew to Istanbul or Beijing just to eat was incredible. Wasteful really. She would not include mangosteen in her order.

When the waiter returned, she was ready. She asked her friends to order first. Hoku chose Japanese. Boring. He was just ordering to go with his hair. Donovan went for quirky, but her choices revealed her as a student of embargo: everything she ordered had been de-listed within the week. Seychelles ordered a watercress salad with black pepper and wild strawberries. This was what came out of her mouth when she opened it, displacing several more ambitious ideas; she was startled. She hoped she hadn't shown it. She steadied herself, thinking: well, that's what I would want to eat. If I ate. The waiter wrote all this down in a beautiful cursive on more of his cotton paper and disappeared.

Seychelles, Rihoku, and Donovan sat elegantly in their mahogany armchairs for a few minutes. They watched the fish. Hoku complained that the humidity from the table was ruining his hair. The waiter returned and silently deposited some small cards on their floating trays, conveying by some indefinable gravity that this was a signal honor. The three eighteen-year-olds looked at each other in puzzlement and rising incredulity. The waiter remained by their table like a wound-down clockwork from an eighteenth-century castle. Seychelles reached for one of the small white cards. It was blank. She flashed it to Donovan with trembling fingers. "*Carte blanche*. It's the chef's card. We can—we can order anything, right?" She turned uneasily to the silent waiter. He nodded.

"Why have you brought these to us?" asked Seychelles, in amazement.

"It is Mr. Arar's privilege," replied the waiter. This unforthcoming answer increased the enormity of it. Seychelles thought of her simpleminded strawberry order. Had it been such a gaffe that this response was a test of their quality? Would they be thrown out if they ordered badly now? People had been thrown out, she knew, and presumably it was not because they were drunk. Deprived of the list of entrée ingredients that she had been expecting, Seychelles was suddenly at sea. She focused her mind on the wavering green fronds half-hidden by her floating tray and felt lost. She nodded.

"Please thank him for us," supplied Donovan. Hoku managed a weak smile. Seychelles knew he would have preferred the standard menu. He did not seek out stress. Donovan would already be calculating out all the angles. It was so unexpected that Seychelles could not work out what she thought of it herself. The waiter nodded to her, ignoring Donovan, and departed once more.

"What do we do now?" asked Hoku.

"We wing it," said Seychelles. Trying to foster some *esprit de corps*, she gave her one bit of advice: "Just think of something you'd really like to eat. Anything."

"But there isn't anything I'd like to eat," said Hoku, "That's the whole point of the bypass." Donovan looked at him as if he'd said something indelicate.

"The point of a bypass is that you can eat absolutely anything you want and it won't matter," she retorted. "I wonder what happens if we order stuff he can't get?"

"Our order's free," joked Seychelles. Donovan looked strategic. "No," continued Seychelles, "I don't think it works that way. I think we order stuff that would be interesting to eat—or to make, right, it's the chef's card—and that, uh, reflects us. It's a form of self-expression." Donovan was bent on finding the right self to express. Hoku was sure that his food-self wasn't going to be as beautiful as his face. Seychelles decided that if she thought about it too much she was going to get nervous and spoil her birthday. "You two," she said, "I'm starting to stress out. I'm just going to take a little walk around. Might as well see the fabulous people, anyway."

Hoku looked affronted. "You got your puffer?" asked Donovan, concerned.

"Yeah." She stood up and moved away from the table, trying not to look aimless. She could hardly say she was going to the bathroom. There were no bathrooms. She went to the windows instead. She threaded her way through the glowing pools of Lucite and the fabulous people sitting around them;

they looked bleached by the white light. The reflections that met her in the silvery tinted windows were even more ethereal; she was reminded of the translucent fish fluttering beneath her menu. The restaurant was an aquarium. Better tell Hoku not to order sashimi, she thought. She smiled at her shatterproof enlightened self in the glass and turned back, passing a dimly-lit wall of glass brick behind which coppery shapes showed in distorted stretches: the kitchen? There was a kitchen, she had read, relic of the restaurant's past in which ordinary food had been prepared: never much of it, and at exorbitant cost, but still, food.

Arar had led the way into the no-food dining era; that was back in the day before the procedure, when food was still dangerous. He was the first one to appreciate its danger and the remedy for it: at his restaurant you could have the pleasure of commanding every kind of food you could imagine without the threat of having to eat it. At first, she had heard, people had ordered spectacular dishes, and the chef had made them; the staff brought them out for you to see and then took them away again. Soon people began to object to the smell, and some wondered what became of the meals; the chef assured them they were safely thrown out, but no one felt certain, so he dispensed with the display altogether, to higher customer satisfaction. Since the advent of the total gastric bypass, the restaurant had become even more fashionable—it was new again, with a different meaning. In principle, Arar could now be serving whatever toxic feasts his patrons dreamed up, knowing it could not hurt them, but people admired the purity of his resolve. He was a true artist.

Seychelles returned to the table. "There," she said, "I've worked up my appetite." The other two looked at her in mild horror. "Just kidding," she said. But she wasn't kidding. As she had walked around the restaurant, she had been asking herself: what is it people want here? What do I want? Her body did not give her hunger signals, but the place did. A scentless, invisible aura of desire pervaded the room. Seychelles understood, as her friends did not, that she had an opportunity to be the chef's perfect customer, the ideal diner. She sat down again, gazing at her wobbly Lucite feet. "All ready?" she asked.

"No," said Hoku.

"Not really," said Donovan, her face still working, crossing off lists in her mind. Her hands were twitching in her lap. Seychelles remembered her habit of drumming her fingers on the table, which was impossible here. Her estimation of Arar rose: he knew how to make things difficult.

Her friends failed to rise to the chef's standard. Hoku did indeed order sashimi, yellowtail, with wasabi, ginger, and mayonnaise. The waiter's eyes glinted at this last detail. Seychelles thought it was with approval, but Hoku was paranoid: "My grandmother always served it that way," he blurted out. The waiter wrote it down with his beautiful cursive. Donovan ordered a complex dish with three kinds of seafood, two of which were illegal, wild boar sausage, rice, and saffron; it also required a certain kind of Spanish wine in the sauce of which there were fewer than 200 bottles left in the world, as Donovan knew because one of them was in her father's cellar. The waiter wrote all this down expressionlessly.

Seychelles took a long, calm breath. She remembered being cold as she stepped into the helicopter; her birthday was in late autumn. The celebrated maple tree on campus had turned, and all its red leaves had been collected. She had hers vacuum-framed in her room, along with the one from the previous year. She quickly ordered braised short ribs of beef with caramelized onions and a mashed yellow potato. Then she smiled hugely with relief and a strange delight at her choice, which had come to her out of the blue; she had only eaten beef twice in her life.

"It's slow," she said, "but I can afford to wait." The waiter smiled. He wrote her order down and headed away toward the translucent wall that suggested, but did not reveal, the kitchen's coppery shapes.

Shortly after that, a door opened soundlessly in the glass brick, and a figure dressed all in white like an ancient magus walked out in soft shoes. It was the chef. He walked silently across the restaurant to their table. The waiter followed him in the hush that had settled over the room and conjured a mahogany chair for him from nowhere that Seychelles could see. He sat down.

"Mr. Arar?" said Seychelles. She was shocked. The chef looked exhausted. He also looked old, which was the truly shocking thing. He was very tall and very thin—too thin, she thought, something she could not recall ever thinking before. He had a nose that in anybody else would have cried out for surgery. His eyes were red-rimmed. Though he was still, agitation hung in the air about him. Seychelles nearly handed him her puffer. He looked at her intensely with his black eyes.

"TGB?" he said in a near-whisper.

"Yes," said Seychelles.

"You ordered those ribs?"

"Yes," said Seychelles.

"Why?"

"It's my birthday."

"Happy birthday," said Arar after a moment. She felt that this automatic phrase was endowed with some astonishing force. She had just been reborn. The congratulatory image of her own father, perfected, pale, provident, seeing her into the helicopter collapsed in her mind like a house of cards. "Do you always eat something special on your birthday?" continued Arar in his hoarse voice.

"Not usually, no. I've been TGB for a while. But this is a restaurant, isn't it?"

"This is a restaurant. Yes," said Arar. He seemed to lack the strength to go on.

"And I thought it would taste nice," said Seychelles, gently, to the thin man staring into the depths of their table. Arar lifted his burning eyes; she was surprised the water was not boiling.

"You thought that?" he said.

"Yes. That it would taste nice," said Seychelles. Her friends looked at each other. They had no idea what was going on. The chef suddenly extended his thin hand across the table, over the bobbing balsa wood, to Seychelles. Some of the tense wrinkles around his eyes smoothed out; he looked younger.

"Hardwicke Arar," he said, his rough voice gaining life. "You may call me Hardy."

The formality of his tone made her conscious of a great privilege. "Thank you," she said. "Seychelles Xenobarbus." She found they were still holding hands over the floating pool of the table. The chef's hand was dry. Something made her press her hand down, still holding Arar's, until it just broke the surface of the water. The wooden trays rocked and the fish scattered in fright. He looked down at their clasped hands, and suddenly pushed them down harder, all the way to the bottom of the tank, soaking her sleeve and her watch. No matter; it was waterproof. She laughed. The chef smiled suddenly and let go her hand, bringing his own out of the water and shaking off the drops. Hoku flinched away from the flying droplets, fearing fish poop.

"Would you like to see the kitchen?" asked Arar, standing up. The waiter's flicker of emotion was as evident as if he had fainted.

"Yes, of course," replied Seychelles. "I walked by it before. I didn't know if it was still in use." She rose, and the chef took her arm. They walked across the floor between tables of gaping people.

"It's a meditation chamber now," said Arar. He led her through the glass-brick door. A large room was revealed to her, full of chrome machinery and copper pans hanging in neat rows. A large empty space was cleared in the center, and a white futon lay on the floor in the precise middle. Seychelles turned slowly. Most of the hardware she had never seen before.

"This is all still here?" she said, "From before?"

"Yes," said Arar, with finality. He looked down at her. "If I were to make those ribs," he asked solemnly, "would you eat them?"

Seychelles looked back at him with equal solemnity. "Yes," she said.

The Last Supper

Hardy died.

Seychelles was just forty; she couldn't bear it. All in all she was likely to live for another sixty years minimum. She was healthy; she was TGB; she had a medical annuity of almost half a billion. She could afford doctors as long as there were any on earth. She would have killed herself except it seemed like such a huge waste of money. Her parents had attributed so much value to her life that she had to keep it intact. After the accident in Santa Monica—the Playhouse Nuke, as the headlines had screamed—they had not even let her visit for fear of exposure; they had never come home but died of radiation sickness in the sanatorium in California. Her father had called it the Nuclear Hotel; it had been a standing joke for the short time they had remained alive. After they were gone Seychelles was worth billions. It was their money; she could not abandon her last link with them. That's it, Hardy, too cheap to die, she thought in grim agony.

Hardy had always gone along with her ludicrous wealth. Until she had met him she had not even realized how ludicrous it was. He had pointed out to her in his more astringent moments that the money she had already cost—in education, in surgery, in security—could support a whole city; her projected life expenses could buy half a continent. She could have all her cells gold-plated individually. There was no end to the ridiculousness that much money could cause: she was dwarfed by it. The wonder of it is, Seychelles, he had said, that despite the buying power of nations you remain just one girl, and I love you. Seychelles was not the richest of her circle of friends, and she had never thought like this before. He had made her think on a different scale. But he had loved her, and that was the second reason she did not kill herself: she could not do away with something that Hardwicke Arar, greatest chef of his generation, had loved.

When she looked down the faceless corridor of her life without him, the one thing she could not see herself getting through was the dinner hour.

He had died at home in her private hospital. On the day of his death, she remembered, she had sent the staff away: the medical officer, the nurses, cleaners, and all. She had left him lying propped on the severe white bed with its pristine linen sheets—he was always a stickler for whites—and wandered around the rest of the house. She had not contacted the undertaker, the lawyer, or the psychiatrist waiting for her call. She had not called her friends. By seven that evening she had been starving, sick and faint with hunger. So it had seemed to her, though she knew she could not be, because of the bypass. Hunger had been cut out of her when she was sixteen.

Still, by the end of that awful day she was famished, a pale and shaking visage in her bathroom mirror: her stomach, or something in the place where her stomach had been, was rumbling. Hunger was the metaphor her body had chosen for grief. There was no gainsaying it. She went to the kitchen, Hardy's beautiful kitchen, and fixed scrambled eggs with chives, brown toast, chanterelles. She put them on one of his white plates and went back to his room. He lay there quietly, his long hands still on the turned-back sheet, his eyes closed, his head tilted back as if inhaling the smell of her mushrooms. He did not argue with her about salting them. She ate everything. She did not speak to him. She would have felt stupid talking to a corpse.

Hardy had always made her hungry. He had taught her to eat before he taught her to cook. Total gastric bypass was irreversible—or not safely reversible, which came to the same thing, it had never been indemnified—or she would have gone back for him. He was not TGB, though by the time he met her almost all his clients at the restaurant were. So he actually lived on his own food. This was so unfashionable it was almost obscene. He did not discuss it in public. But the amazing thing about him from the beginning, from her first meeting him at NoFood the day she was eighteen, was the way in which his cooking—the very idea of his cooking—restored to her the sensory demand of which she had been deprived.

She did not need any food at all, except Hardy's. From sixteen to eighteen she had hardly eaten. But from the moment she had risen to his challenge and eaten the meal he had cooked her (short ribs, they still had them every year on her birthday), that powerful feeling, hunger, had come back to her in all of its urgency. That first evening she had felt it so strongly, and it was so alien, that she feared she was having some kind of breakdown; she had come near to overdosing on her puffer from anxiety and had been completely tranquilized at the table. Hardy had overlooked her drugged docility and served her food anyway, and the shock of it had broken through her torpor: not just the taste but the satiety. No longer accustomed to feeling either empty or full, the satisfaction was totally unexpected.

She had spoken to psychologists about it afterward: the effect was classed as a phantom sensation, suffered by a small percentage of the TGBers. Her surgeon was apologetic: there were therapies. Seychelles said nothing but went home laughing. She was not suffering. Hardy had given her back the truth, and she did not care that it was a medical impossibility. Hardy was a magician.

Over the twenty-two years they had been together, perhaps her initial euphoria had cooled, but never entirely. As she matured and came to understand herself, she learned that it was her love for Hardy that caused her hunger and repletion, mapping the ebb and flow of her desire and admiration. It *was* a phantom sensation, stronger than a real one. Her worry soon became that she could inspire no similar hunger in Hardy. He got hungry, he ate; it had nothing to do with her. It was heartless. She schooled herself into reading his love for her by other means, but always felt in this strangely his superior, constantly giving herself over to the enormous involuntary power of her love for him in a way he could not reciprocate.

On the other hand, she also felt that there were ways in which she could never get close to Hardy, though he could to her: chiefly, he digested her food. The things she made for him became part of him. Her love was in his flesh. This was not true for her. Hardy's beautiful food never touched any part of her flesh but her mouth and her anus; otherwise it passed through bioflex tubing.

By the time she had finished her chanterelles that evening, though, anger was growing inside her. It made her desolate to think that it was the only thing that could grow inside her. That had ever grown inside her. She had not been able to bear Hardy's child.

At first, of course, she had assumed that this was perfectly normal, part of the order of things. Women who could afford TGB—which was everyone she knew—were spared the risk and demeaning and timewasting labor of carrying their own children. Their uteruses had been excised along with everything else, removing forever the chances of vile gynecological cancers, humiliating fatness, and career interruption.

Yet when she was about to set up the standard VF surrogacy, thaw a few eggs, Hardy came over all panicky. She was confused. She had always known he was a purist, had weird retro notions, but had imagined that they were confined to eating.

"Hardy, love, come on, this isn't a food thing. This is our child we're talking about."

"Oh God. Yes, I know. I just didn't think—you mean all that's gone, too? I thought it was bad enough at the restaurant, catering to that spooky shunt that runs through everyone, and now —"

He tried repeatedly to make the standard donation so she could set up the surrogacy, but for over a year emerged from bathrooms, bedrooms, and clinics pale, clammy, and retching.

"I can't do it," he said, finally, humiliated.

Seychelles had stared at him in despair. "Hardy, why? I just don't get it. It takes two minutes."

"No, it's not that—well, yes it is—but I can't stand the thought of the baby growing outside you, being fertilized outside you, stored eggs, ugh, like caviar—sorry—and then fastening itself inside somebody else like a parasite—"

"You'd rather have the parasite inside me, then?"

"Yes!"

"Would you want it inside you?"

"Yes! Yes! Rather than a stranger. Yes! It would be my child then. Ours. In substance and design. Is there some way—?"

"So it's not our baby if it doesn't eat us, Hardy?"

He was silent. "Yes," he whispered. She had walked out. They had not spoken—and she had not eaten—for two years. He had closed NoFood and gone on a trip to the Asias, falling dangerously ill for eight months in Taipei. "Just my luck the borders had re-opened that year, isn't it?" he said shamefacedly afterward. But he had not come home with any fresh conviction of the superiority of civilized life and the benefits it conferred, such as the equality of the person that Seychelles believed she was assuming in divesting herself of her uterus.

He had seen pregnant women in the hospital.

"They were in the hospital, Hardy," she could not resist saying, "They were sick. They were at risk."

"True," he admitted. "But they looked happy."

"You didn't see them in labor."

He jerked his head in assent but could say nothing. They had one final argument about it, but it was an exhausted one. They had fought slowly around the circle until he had interrupted with:

"So what about the surrogate?"

"What about her?"

"How is she made equal by your operation?"

"She isn't."

"Then how can you talk about the equality of the person? You mean the equality of rich people who can afford surgeons."

"Hardy, I don't care about her!" she had shouted. "I care about me! I don't care: not everybody can afford equality!"

He had remained stubbornly silent, letting this close their exchange. By means of this cheap trick—it was a cheap trick, she maintained—he had got the better of her. Her own angry shout echoed in her mind. It was not that she developed radical empathy for the surrogate, whoever she might have been, and she didn't think Hardy had any either. He was just desperate. He did not believe in the new kind of person that she was, and it was his misfortune that he loved her anyway. She saw herself through Hardy's eyes, not as modern, enhanced, stripped down, safe, but as violated. Everything about her missing guts terrified him. He loved the outside of her but could not bring himself to think about her insides. All this had left a crimp in their sex life for years.

Consequently, she was alone when he died, and it was all his fault. She put down her knife and fork with trembling hands and stared at him lying there complacently. Hardy, you stubborn bastard, she thought, I could be sitting here with our ten-year-old.

He had been the gutless one.

Day two crawled by. She still had not called the authorities, the coroner, whatever, and was getting anxious about germs. Hardy was still lying in his bed. He had left no funeral directions. By evening she was once again starving.

She prepared a more elaborate meal this time: chicken stew with raisins, saffron rice, spiced fava beans. She popped the beans out of their casings one at a time. There was no need to hurry. Hardy had hated to hurry his cooking; it was the legacy of a lifetime in restaurants, always in a rush. It was one reason the no-food concept had appealed to him: if you don't actually serve any food, no one will rush you. You can unfold the intricacies of menu planning unpressured by all the last-minute crises of meal preparation. At home, while cooking real food, he proceeded with a kind of willful slowness. Dinner had regularly taken three hours to prepare.

Seychelles could not equal him; she was done in less than two and a half.

On the third night she decided to try a recipe she had never made before. It required some specialized ingredients. Normally she would have ordered them in but instead went out herself to get them; she didn't want anybody else in the house. Hardy would wait for her.

She went to Bernini and Fiasco's and got what she wanted, some capers and morels, the latter only on the strength of Hardy's influence with the proprietor, as they had recently been re-listed. Wild mycelia everywhere now were heavily guarded due to some interest they had raised among machine geneticists: something to do with models for distributed sentience, Donovan had told her. Seychelles was past caring about this. She loved mushrooms.

Donovan had followed her father's footsteps into embargo and was always up-to-date on the lists. All the time Seychelles and Hardy were operating Floating Island, the private catering business that had succeeded NoFood, they had kept a hotline to her office: they had prided themselves on compliance. Donovan could have got them off of anything, she was the smartest lawyer around, but they felt that the power of their timely information—the lists changed hourly—was more impressive than defiance. It was hard to keep Donovan convinced of this, however. She was a pugilist and an epicure. She had been a founding member of Floating Island, supper club of the super elite. Their first event had been at her place downtown.

Seychelles came home from Fiasco's, opened all the doors that separated the kitchen from the hospital wing, and began her tasks of chopping and blending. A delicious smell percolated through the house. She worked for three and a half hours. The dish was a success. She carried it proudly through the aromatic halls to Hardy's room and ate it beside him, in her familiar chair. He had never been fond of Mediterranean food, but she felt this was a time to strike out on her own. Maybe she was nervous about this piece of independence, however; she spilled a bit of tomato-fennel broth on the corner of his white bed as she sat down.

She could hardly take her eyes off it as she ate.

All night she worried about that little red stain on Hardy's bed. She knew he would have hated it. He always kept at least three sets of whites handy in the kitchen, even at home. Things were getting out of hand.

She got out of bed, unslept and ragged, in the early morning and called the lawyer. He was not surprised at her call but was surprised at her request. He would take care of everything. She should take care of herself after all the strain, call her psychiatrists, he would look after it.

Seychelles went to Donovan's place for two days. Though Donovan cooked for her, cooked like the gastronome she was, charter member of the most exclusive dining club ever to exist, Seychelles couldn't eat. She reminisced about Hardy, used her puffer a lot, and cried. Donovan held her hand as they sat together on a couch of illegal leather and peered out over the lights of the city and the occasional passing helicopter through their bloodshot eyes.

When Seychelles returned home, all the doors were neatly closed. The house was pristine. There was a strange smell. It reminded her of cinnamon, and she immediately determined to do some baking. She checked on Hardy in his room. The stain was gone, and the bed was flawlessly made with hospital corners. He reposed quietly there, long hands still on the top of the turned-back sheet, eyes closed, head tilted up as after a long sigh. He looked exactly the same. His coffee-colored skin was smooth, his face thin and taut over its bones, his bird of prey nose jutted up proudly.

She immediately felt the need for a snack.

Smiling, she went to the kitchen, leaving all the doors open behind her. A while later she returned with mace-and-nutmeg scones, cheddar and pears, some Earl Grey tea. She laid these on the small white table that had appeared there. She sat and ate them in a kind of distant contentment, watching Hardy's face. She planned her menus for the week.

Gringo

Gringo was a pig. He had been working for Procurements International for seven years; he was a Gatherer: PIG. He was proud of it. He had started in Central America just after the war, gathering green spiky plants from some river down there. He had been amazed to find it still had rivers; he had thought it was all desert. It mostly was, but not all. A lot of the water had been fast frozen and transported for damages, but there was some left. Enough to be of interest to a pharmaceutical buyer who had sent him down there to crawl through shallow muddy water protected by snipers to bring back specimens of whatever that grass was: it had cut up his hands, the only part of him not protected by his camouflage wetsuit. An over-sight, but it had been his first job. He'd never even learned the correct name of the stuff he was looking for then, just the Spanish word, whatever that was; he couldn't recall. All Spanish sounds the same.

Now he made a point of knowing the right names for things; it looked professional. It helped him to keep a run-ning tally in his mind of all the delicacies and desirables he had found all over the world for the people who needed them at home. What you want, you need. If you can afford it, you need it; otherwise, you can just want it. Whatever. This was the kind of stuff he thought up on planes.

This time it was mushrooms: morels, *morchella deliciosa,* specifically, the sexual organs of a branching underground structure called a mycelium. Nature was so disgusting: lop off its genitals and they just grow back. They were found in three places in the world, two in Italy and one in southern France.

So he was in France. Apparently these mycelium things were hundreds of years old; the one he was headed for was older than the second republic; it had been around in the days of steam engines and television. Billions of people had died since then, and here it was, still living its pointless life. Nature. Fucking pave it.

It was one of the satisfactions of his work that he got to steal things from the wilderness, the bits that were left, though rarely enough to do significant damage. If he could have, he would have blown it up behind him each time. There was a lot of dying going on, and he couldn't see why the grubs and shrubs shouldn't come in for their share.

He sat in his hotel room and contemplated strategy. He had thought about infiltrating one of the universities involved but decided against it; with nothing to do but whatever it was they did, the scientists would have too much time to ask questions. He had gotten by quite well various times in the industrial sector where everybody was kept too busy to notice much. A simple clipboard sufficed. He had some fake ID from the Stanford-Montpellier Sentience Group that was running this project but did not expect it to do anything except get him past some security, and probably not even that. They had defense funding.

He would never pass muster as a researcher. His only hope of getting near a scientist was to pretend to be an accountant. Accountants are the only group scientists fear. He put it out of his mind and surveyed his equipment. He had enough tactical and surveillance gear to assassinate a small-time president. His job was much more important than that, though: it was to get people what they want, exactly what they want, from anywhere on earth. He was the avenging angel, bucking all the embargoes and rationalizations and fears, bringing people what they desired.

He decided to work at night, as he nearly always did. Even the best security is not as good in the dark, and he hated sleeping anyway. He put on his camerasuit and walked around the town; there was little he could learn from casual talk, as he spoke no French. Sitting around with a translator and no companion was too obvious. You had to have a good reason to risk traveling, and that reason was usually business, which you don't do alone. It wasn't like people were just wandering around admiring the scenery after passing through four security cordons and with at least two known pandemic strains in the area.

He made it to the edge of the wood, looking at this and that, his suit recording everything; he examined the security fencing that began a few paces into the tree cover—not much cover, the trees were widely and symmetrically spaced, uniform in height and smoothness, with small green-yellow leaves making a high, light canopy—and tried to determine how many men were on duty. It appeared to be seven. They did not look especially attentive, but they were armed to the teeth and had the new spectrum sensors.

The fenced area was not large and had no signage. Everyone in town already knew why they were there, if not exactly what they were doing. There were two small white buildings inside, probably portable labs. The guards spoke English; they had been hired from the Stanford end of things, unsurprisingly. This meant they would be better than locals, but also undoubtedly that they hated the locals, and vice versa, and probably also their university masters. The simplest way in would probably be through one of them. He hung around for a while so they would note him and spoke into his suitlink so they heard him speak English. Then he left.

He walked back through the town at dusk. The weird thing about France was that it was full of restaurants—on the streets, in the squares, right out in public. People all around him were eating at these restaurants, sitting in the open air; he could see the food on their plates, smell cooking odors spreading from open doors. It made him gag. He supposed most of them had had the operation, but they still did it. The French were like that, he had heard. This was where all the mushrooms had gone before, presumably. The whole idea of eating fungi was sickening. He hurried through the lit-up streets to his hotel.

He let a day elapse. The next night, late, he went back to the woods, not wearing any gear or disguise, and loitered by the dark perimeter. After about half an hour, one of the guards came over. "Hi," he said neutrally.

"Hi," said Gringo neutrally.

"What are you here for?"

"Morels," said Gringo.

"Who do you work for?"

"Procurement."

"Whatcha offering?"

"Fully hopped-up medicharge card; no strings; military. Priority access to all the vaccines." It was true; he had one. It was his, but he had no use for vaccines. The guard was interested, though. He was a young, strong, fit guy, in love with his body and afraid for it, like everyone who worked in hot zones. He grunted in assent, made a just-a-minute gesture, and walked away. A moment later he was back.

"I can get you five," he said, "from the lab. That's all that's above ground at the moment. They might be treated, though, sprayed with something, I don't know."

"Fine. Thanks," said Gringo. The man was being honest about things. He let him speak.

"Come back tomorrow night," said the guard. "Ask for Michael."

"Thanks," said Gringo again, and walked out of the forest. The guard watched him go. Gringo came back the next night, handed the card through the fence, and duly received a small white paper bag with a code on it, its top neatly folded over and clipped. Inside were five ugly objects like freeze-dried penises with a faint earthy smell.

"They may be marked in some way," warned the guard, "check 'em. They were real upset in the lab. Madeleine, the head, she actually cried. Scientists are weird. You want to be careful. I can get you more in a few days. There's a new crop coming."

"Excellent," said Gringo. "I'm always careful with shipments," he added soberly.

"Do they train you and all?"

"Yes," said Gringo. "Thinking of changing sides?"

"Well," said the guard, "what do I care about spores and computers and shit? They're just mushrooms; if people want to eat them, let them. Seems more normal to me."

"Does it?"

"People will pay a ton for these things."

"True. They will. The things people want to eat amaze me."

"Well, they do smell bad," the guard admitted. "Come back Wednesday."

Gringo made three trips back to see Michael and by trading one more black market medicard and some high-delivery nutrient strips, also military, obtained seven more mushrooms. He scanned them every way he could think of and then shipped them out by company courier. His account balances rose nicely. The fourth time he went back, all the personnel had changed; they were bristling and aggressive and shouted him off. Gringo wondered if Michael was still contemplating an alternate career in procurement, and if so, from what venue. He wished him well.

He was at liberty to go home now. But then, he was always at liberty. He decided to make one practical run before leaving. So far the job had not been taxing, and he felt he should be working harder for his money. Also, exhaustion was beneficial to him; he slept deeply afterward. He had been far too relaxed in France, and all those restaurants were getting to him, people's jaws going up and down; the dream was returning.

He had managed to keep it at bay since the sumach trip to Turkey. It was part of the fundo bloc: purdah had made everything too easy. Sumach was readily available in the markets, and after he'd bought practically a ton of it in three different towns he was getting antsy and needed a challenge. He longed to be arrested. The dream had come back with a vengeance, and having his hands cut off would have been a welcome distraction.

He had been so crazy he had thought of going home and having them surgically removed, and maybe a few other parts as well, or all of them, everything except his head, which could be kept in a jar somewhere, remembering, remembering. He cried and shook for five hours on the flight home. It was a company plane so nobody saw.

In his tasteful white hotel room in the south of France he lay in his bed fighting sleep. In the end he could not do without it completely. Without food, yes, but not without sleep. There was no way to excise it. Not yet. When there was, he would be first in line.

His eyes closed, and Margret came, as she always did, standing across the stream. They were in a bright green meadow dotted with flowers. There were few things he hated more than this meadow. She was sixteen: beautiful, brown-haired, and young, with plump limbs, wearing a white hospital gown. "Hi, dad. Here I am," she said, with quiet reproof, as if he had been temporarily ignoring her in some paternal distraction, gently, as if he did not spend his whole conscious life denying this returning encounter. "How are you?" she asked.

He had started out answering this question with "fine." Then, with more honesty, he had answered it with "terrible." Then with rending outbursts of weeping, screaming, hysterical pounding and kicking of the ground and sky. He had tried repeatedly to cross the stream, to touch and hold his daughter, and he never could. Now he answered her laconically, stoically, with "I'm still here." This acknowledgement of his own place within the dream steadied him. It was a distancing strategy. He had also found that this admission stilled the landscape, which lessened the disorientation, although it focused his attention more on Margret and so increased the pain.

Still, plain ordinary pain—the straight agony of loss, like thoracic surgery without anesthetic—was better than the nausea he had suffered from those mixed emotions and fears that flickered through the landscape when it was alive. The worst was the stream: during the years when he had been fighting and fighting to cross it, it had morphed horribly, shrinking and widening, changing into a river of blood, into stinking black fluid, into a mass of pale waving wormlike tubes. He had seen faces in it; he had seen food; he had waded in excrement up to his ankles and never been able to cross to her. He had learned not to fight the dream itself.

He knew that there was some part of him that required the dream. He saw her so clearly in it, so perfect, virtual, not at all in the way in which she occurred in his memory. Memory is crap. We remember only our own feelings about people, not them at all. Everything but them, in fact. Margret appeared in the dream as an insult, or maybe an antidote, to his whole normal way of recalling her, showing every time not only what he had lost but how inadequate were his usual resources for reconstructing her.

"How are you?" he asked, inevitably.

"Fine," she answered, beaming, "great, you know. Looking forward to it." It was not that his heart sank, or even froze, but more that it was covered with a thin tightening film. The one time he had used an oral security polymer, fearing poisoning by illegal animal traders in China as he was looking for boar's tongue, he had experienced the sensation of the inside of his mouth shrinking two sizes instantly. The feeling had been eerily familiar.

Beautiful sixteen-year-old Margret, happy, unknowing, looked forward to her bypass, guarantor of acceptability and cool. It had been her graduation present. All her friends had it: TGB. He himself had it, so did everyone he knew. It was standard. Safe. Total gastric bypass had eliminated at a stroke all the diseases of human digestion: no guts, no cancer; no food, no obesity; no blood sugar, no diabetes. All of it, solved by advanced blood chemistry and surgery. The huge waste of time that was eating and excreting was over, for him and his family and everyone who could afford it. His daughter deserved it.

Margret was an exceptional girl. Everyone agreed she was gifted; she had already been admitted into the most prestigious college in the city. She was exceptionally charming, sweet natured, pretty, modest in a generation of gasbags. Exceptional.

She came through surgery fine, no trauma, came through post-op well. Two months later she began to reject her nutrient batches. She had tested normally before TGB, met all the criteria. Her reaction was exceptionally rare. She was one of a handful of cases ever recorded. They switched her from batch to batch through all the major suppliers, and finally into previous generations of nutrients; eventually she showed allergy to them all. Her blood would not carry the chemical support it needed.

Her body was covered with permanently swollen injection sites; she became skeletal. She needed fresh blood to stay alive, but after they had transfused all the surplus volume of her own stored after the surgery, she began rejecting blood from donors. Gringo had been the main one; they had been the same type. Her body finally refused even her father's blood, and she had died of nutrient starvation just short of her seventeenth birthday. The lovely Margret who stood before him across the brief span of the running water, the fluttering white strings of her gown coming untied, did not look a thing like the emaciated form of the girl he had finally known.

She spoke to him from that morning, the morning of the surgery—a clear day like this one, in spring—brave and bright, the catheter already in her arm. His wife had killed herself almost immediately after Margret's death. He did not blame her. He would have done the same, except that then there would have been nobody left to remember her, not as she deserved. None of her stupid little friends could do it, not with their flimsy love, not her useless boyfriend. Her mother was gone. It had to be him. He was all the posterity she had.

So he stood up again from where he had fallen on his knees on the wet bank and he said: "Margret, I'm sorry, so sorry, you must know that I love you more than anything else in the world, and I'm sorry we did it, sorry we let you go through with it." He had said these words so often they had become a mantra. She smiled and looked at him uncomprehendingly.

"Dad," she said, "don't worry. I think you're more worried than I am."

He wanted to end their futile conversation, but at the same time every word he said kept her longer in front of his eyes.

"Margret," he said, "I don't know where you are, or why we're here, or anything. But we keep coming back here, to the water. I have to leave you again and again. It's awful, Margret."

She smiled at him valiantly and said, "Dad, you worry too much. It's all going to be fine."

These parallel conversations could go on and on. It seemed to him that her range of responses was narrowing each time he had the dream now, becoming more automatic. She said less and less, and he looked at her more and more. There was something about this Margret that was like that: silent and pure. She was the missing Margret he could never capture in his memories, which were just moods and flashes of motion. He was content just to look at her, to hold her in his mind.

The dream ended with the two of them staring across at each other without speaking, under the bright sun, separated by the flowing stream. He woke with tears in his eyes, as usual.

He began to clean his guns. It was still dark. He could go out now. His weapons shot fine tranquilizer barbs, not bullets; he didn't shoot to kill. He had never killed anyone on a job. Maybe one Mexican. He pulled on a full spectrum camouflage suit under his clothes—the things were incredibly hot when covered with exterior fabric, but he could just make it to the edge of the woods. He packed all his gear and sensors in an ultralight bag. He had no plan. There wasn't much room for a plan given the variables—not much beyond being very, very quiet around seven armed men. He knew he was wigged out from the dream, but his need for action was acute.

He walked through the town in the dark, past the hateful restaurants at last empty in the wee hours, trying not to rush and overheat in his suit. He stripped off as soon as he was in shadow and waited to cool down. He blacked his face. He readied his bag for the specimens. He hoped he wouldn't squish them too much getting them out. That was the whole point of it, wasn't it, Operation Morel, that he should get these precious mushrooms out whole? Who knows why people want these things so badly? Why should they not have them? They were things that could be had.

Why should the Department of Embargo or the Stanford-Montpellier Sentience Group be able to tell us what we can or cannot have? That was why he worked in procurement. What most people need is a little relief.

He worked his way slowly to the fence. He burned a small hole in the alloy with his microlite; he hated using them because they made a spark, but nothing else would cut security fencing. He wormed his way through and crept silently to the nearest tree. Apparently the mycelium spread through all the ground underneath the protected part of the forest; the mushrooms could spring up anywhere, and they typically grew around the bases of the trees. He felt carefully around the base of his tree for any growths. There were none. He moved to the next tree. None. He could see fairly well in the dark with his lenses, but he found his first mushroom, at the third tree, by smell. It had never occurred to him that he could work by smell, but he smelled it clearly in the dark.

Mushrooms prefer dark, so there were no lights anywhere. He found three more mushrooms in a cluster at a fourth tree; they were wafting clearly since he was so low to the ground. The earthy, fishy smell filled his nose. Maybe he inhaled too loudly. At the fifth tree, sniffing along, Gringo was shot in the back by security.

He died instantly, almost soundlessly, his four morels still in his hand. These were taken away and labeled carefully as R4A, B, C, and D, where they played their small part in the data set that led to the development of the first fungiform network, Sporenet.

Gringo they left lying there till morning. What was one dead pig, more or less?

Cakes and Ale

Dost thou think that because thou art virtuous, there
shall be no more cakes and ale?

— Falstaff, *Henry IV*, Part 2

The first serious restaurant Hardwicke Arar worked in
was Cakes and Ale. He was sous-chef. It was a nightmare,
but he learned a lot. Abundance was their thing. It was about
presenting copious amounts of food gorgeously. They went
for platters. The look of the place was Elizabethan, with real
half-timbering and dark panels: all the wood was illegal, and
this was characteristic of the operation. They served whatever
they wanted, regardless of its list status, and were constantly
involved in litigation. This did not bother Sue and Peg, who
owned the restaurant; they considered it part of the normal
cost of business. Hardy, on the ground in the kitchen, spent
half his time filling out forms. The embargo reps were always
there, and the cost of feeding them was enormous. Hardy
thought it was stupid, a serious distraction from his true calling.

He was twenty at the time. He found his youth annoy-
ing. Sue and Peg beamed upon him because he was genuinely
young as opposed to surgically altered, like them and most
of the clientele. "You're so delicious, Hardy," they would say:
"the real thing. Not like us old haddocks." Neither of them

looked a day older than he did. He was tall and gawky, with a nose that mounted a constant attack on the world, the only feature of which he felt proud. He had heard Sue and Peg discussing his nose: I wonder when he'll give in and get it fixed?

He would never get it fixed. It wasn't broken, and he needed it for cooking. He walked around behind his nose as if it were a banner held in front of him, announcing his status of combating everything. Everything. Sue and Peg and their patrons and their assembly-line noses and cheekbones and teeth; the ludicrous amounts of food that they ate, or at least commanded; the menu; the world. He would not give in. Let the world adjust, the infinitely pliable, ageless world.

He stayed at Cakes and Ale for five years, working all hours, cooking everything, putting out fires; he stayed and determinedly got wrinkles. Sue and Peg began to look at him with concern. He cooked better and better; he looked worse and worse. Finally they fired him for insubordination. All that ageing was bad for morale.

With his savings and his severance package— "it's what you need, Hardy, a little severance" they said sniffily—he opened NoFood. He had already attracted a following, a dedicated crowd who came to Cakes and Ale to eat his food and ignore the décor and the ridiculous heaped platters: they ordered appetizers and sat in tight little groups with their backs to the banqueting table. Hardy found the tallest building he could afford, which was pretty tall, 200 floors, respectable—and leased the top suite. Peg and Sue's place had been on the ground. NoFood could only be reached by helicopter.

Soon after he took possession he had the patrons' elevator blocked off, retaining only the small private one for the chef and staff. He ascended to his new restaurant; his clients descended from on high, like birds of prey. As he whizzed up the building in his golden car in the mornings, he felt like a solar deity arising, son of an accountant and a middle manager from suburbia meeting the gods.

For the gods came to NoFood. They came almost immediately. They graced it with their presence and brought along their priests and apparatchiks, while almost wholly misunderstanding the place, as gods do.

For instance, they liked the décor. Hardy hated décor, despised the very notion of décor as a useless distraction from the experience of dining; he kept it severely minimal and changed it every two weeks to illustrate his contempt. It was disposable. To them this expressed the height of fashion. Elliptical aesthetic reasons were proffered for his every change; the restaurant was regularly featured in style magazines. Hardy faced these down with dismissive calm.

He knew, by the time he had been operating NoFood for four years, that he was serving the best food in the world and that almost nobody noticed. There was nothing to do but to maintain his standards and hope that occasionally one among the hordes of celebrities and gourmets would happen to actually taste the food, though he knew it would be a matter of rare conjunction, like an eclipse.

He had begun cooking for his parents, Sarastro and Stella Arar, at the age of ten. Not knowing all that much about food, which was frankly a retro concern, after all, in most people's busy lives, they had simply liked to eat what he prepared and were content to let him experiment.

He had asked for a stove for his twelfth birthday.

"A what?" his mother asked.

"A stove. It's a big metal thing with a door into it, and plates on top of it. You heat the metal up until it's really hot and it cooks the food."

"Just how big is this thing?" asked his mother cautiously.

It was huge. The only one they could find was an antique. For the first couple of months they lived in fear that he would burn the house down. Their insurers were not happy. But Hardy was ecstatic. The stuff he was learning to do was incredible, and he had never heard of most of it anywhere else. He felt like a time traveler, bringing back secrets from the remote past. His parents were mystified but approving.

He discovered Bernini and Fiasco's at age sixteen and persuaded his parents to open an account with them, so that he could work with deluxe ingredients, real animal protein and the like. By the time he was seventeen he was one of the best cooks on the continent, and Bernini himself, the kingmaker, was taking a personal interest.

One day, one horrible day, Hardy was there, downtown, on the 300th floor, negotiating for genuine, sea-grown nori, when one of the flash floods that ripped through the central-western suburbs took out his entire neighborhood, including his house, stove, and both parents. Hardy had hardly felt a ripple. His life had been saved by Japanese seaweed. He had lost Stella and Sarastro, his first, best, and beloved diners.

Bernini took in the devastated boy for several months. He was a prodigious talent and had run up a huge bill. Hardy chopped a lot of onions to disguise his crying jags. Walking in on one of these, Bernini had said to him, rather stiffly: cook for them now, Hardy, cook for them.

So he opened NoFood.

The name of the restaurant had caused him grave concern. He had thought at first of calling it LessFood, but this was temporizing: less than what? Less than the moronic plenty of Cakes and Ale? He did not want to be bound by such antinomies. It was more: let there be no food, if not perfect food. Food in its quintessence—which was another name he considered—perfect in taste, texture, aroma, appearance, proportion, that had nothing to do with cosmetics, surgery, diets, fame, global events, demographic trends, science, or dating. Of course this was impossible: Nobody's Food. Except his. The food of Hardwicke Arar: NoFood. Inimitable. He put that simple name on the exterior wall facing the helipad, on the menus and cards, in the one ad he ever ran to announce the opening venue, and left it to the pundits and reviewers to craft the slogans: There's NoFood Like It, haha.

By the time the restaurant was two years old he had a nineteen-month waiting list. The president of the republic had eaten there; visiting dictators dropped in; gossip columnists, intelligentsia, greeting card manufacturers, CEOs whose net worth was greater than the entire planet, entertainers and infomerchants of every kind, plus their children, flunkies, and guests jostled in his electronic queue to get into NoFood. He served them flawless *porc aux pruneaux* and saffron-lemon pie and made them sit on hard chairs, tagine with olives and raspberry-leaf tea and made them sit on backless ones, beef flank stir-fried with chives and sticky rice while perched on rude seats made from planks.

Only the food was comfortable. Rich women snagged their stockings and did not complain. Arar did not care about their stockings or their opinions. His reputation was ferocious.

He did not do private catering. No matter who was on his guest list, he refused to cook halal, or kosher, or vegetarian, or PanGaia Reformed; religion had no place at his table. Most amazingly of all, he was scrupulous about embargo. His staff knew that he had a pathological hatred of filling out forms, but it was widely felt that Arar's punctilio about the official import lists was part and parcel of his whole personality. His deference to laws that most people paid no attention to was strangely impressive. He had become one of that awkward and compelling class of mavericks who even in their conventional moments are assumed to be conducting Byzantine campaigns of incomprehensible defiance.

By the time he was thirty he was in a serious bind. NoFood's success had outrun itself. People still *in utero* were being added to the waiting list. Hardy's problem, though, was with the food. Glowing reviews poured out of every gastronome worth the name, but who pays attention to restaurant reviews? The last thing they can convey is how the food tastes. Diners said this or that in passing that gave him some hope, but more and more he was stuck in a kind of echoing, doomy sphere of nothingness.

There was one particularly large jar in the kitchen that began to make him panicky; finally he deliberately dropped it. While this provided temporary relief, the problem did not go away. There did not seem to be any way to escape being Hardwicke Arar, creator of food so perfect that it had become invisible. He considered absconding and starting a new restaurant under another name, but this plan would almost inevitably involve surgery, and he continued to object to it on principle. He considered a scorched earth policy of bringing everything to the tables severely burnt just to see if anyone would notice, but he could not do that to his own food. He brooded in the early morning hours after the restaurant closed, writing out menus in stark black longhand, adding and crossing things out as he talked to his embargo lawyer, staring out at the empty helipad. He found himself staring blankly at the quiet lettering on the wall. NoFood. NoFood.

NoFood?

If his wonderful food was invisible—?

People dined out on ideas, so why not just cut to the chase? It was obvious. In his despair at his unloved food, Hardy, as a joke on himself, as what he assumed would be a terminal insult to his customers, suddenly arrived at the no-food concept that was to surge through the world of fashionable dining like a riptide. Its effects are still to be felt in many quarters. National economies have collapsed as the result of it. Arar dolls are still ritually burned at the RealFood Annual General Meeting—though RealFoodists are generally acknowledged to be a bit behind the times—as well as spontaneously by chefs and zealous amateurs around the world. Of course, the momentum of the whole no-food movement was inevitably greatly extended by the advent of TGB, which he could never have anticipated.

Hardy had no idea of such far-reaching consequences as he sat contemplating what he envisioned as his professional suicide; he thought only, grimly, that it would simplify his life on the supply side for the next few days—which is as long as he expected his business to last. It had always been a huge pain to receive provisions by helicopter.

The next morning when the staff came in, Hardy fired them all, all the kitchen help at least. He gave everybody as much severance as he could afford, which was a lot, promised references and interest, and sent them away, keeping only those who did front of house. Chief of these was Carl, his headwaiter, a beautiful man with an automatized calm that Hardy attributed to tranquilizers or some form of surgical intervention.

"Hardy," said Carl in his anesthetic way, "what are you doing?"

"I've decided to stop serving food," replied Hardy heroically. "People don't want it anyway."

"Fantastic," said Carl, calmly.

"So I've prepared a very ambitious menu—six entrees, twelve appetizers—and people can choose among them. That's what they really want to do, choose. Talk. Not eat."

"Great," said Carl.

"So you take down their orders, and—I don't know, commend them? Then go away and after a decent interval for conversation, present them with the bill."

"Right," said Carl.

"Okay?"

"Okay."

Carl never required any more instruction than this. He showed great initiative. In fact, it is doubtful that the no-food scheme would have survived its first few days to become the sensation it did had anyone other than Carl been at the helm.

He did very little commending. He did no explaining or justifying. He was unmoved by ranting, threats, or laughter. He was calm. Under his unrelenting gaze all protest leached away and was replaced by the desire for approval. Hungry or demanding diners undeceived themselves under his eye, seeing through the boring, standard, materialist expectations of the meal they had been anticipating to the enlightened core experience being offered. To the demanding, it was ordering. To the hungry, it was denial. To the educated, it was the chance to have their skill or taste acknowledged. To almost everybody, it was the ritual of choice.

Carl presided over this array of experiences with the same zen authority that he had exerted over the delivery of the regular menu; the unflappable continuity of his presence piloted many regulars, and all the wait staff, through the transition. Within a week the new, literal NoFood was even more famous and subject to even more universal praise than it had been before. Absolutely everyone was struck with the severity, the truth, the unremitting extremeness of this approach: it was pure Arar.

All through the first evening Hardy sat in the empty kitchen and alternately laughed and wept. Carl drifted in serenely from time to time to check on him. Not a single patron stormed out. All night Hardy heard regular levels of restaurant noise coming through the wall—possibly a bit loud, excited, inquiring, but within normal parameters, no more than a particular celebrity or an adjacent bombing would elicit.

"How's it going?" he whispered hoarsely to Carl as he came in for the third time. He could not bring himself to go out and look.

Carl came over and patted his arm and said, with glazed sympathy, "Fine. It's fine. It's all going to be okay."

Nobody missed the food at all.

Hardy, increasingly hysterical and bitterly drinking the excellent wine he was no longer serving to his patrons, embarked on a long, muzzy conversation with Sarastro and Stella's portraits that hung on the kitchen wall. Carl buzzed continuously in and out like a honeyless bee.

"Carl, I'd like you to meet my parents," he said grandly, much later. Carl gazed at the pictures, cleared the bottles away, and put on some tea before disappearing to close up. He came back, carried Hardy to the futon in the back office, and tucked him away, as if folding a napkin.

"What would I do without you, Carl?" muttered Hardy.

"Fall apart," said Carl, turning off the light and settling down on the stained and smoky kitchen couch.

Carl hung around Hardy constantly for those first six weeks of the no-food regime, like a stoned angel. When Hardy seemed stabilized, he asked him for a med leave for a new surgery. Hardy gave it to him and did not enquire further, though he could not think of any part of Carl that had not already been improved. He was a bit shocked at the recovery time: two months. It was evidently something major.

During the time Carl was away, Hardy discovered a certain personal liberation in the no-food concept. He kept the kitchen minimally stocked, reserving the right—which he might spontaneously exercise at any time, though he never did—to cook the food that appeared on his changing menus. The menus he pored over and elaborated with exquisite care. Many of them he cooked in the spirit of experiment, and ate himself, though many he did not. Often the latter, purely hypothetical dishes were among his favorites. He knew exactly how they would taste, how they would look and feel and smell: they had a perfection all their own. Seeing as there was nothing else for it—he knew he could not back away from the no-food concept now—he entered into his quintessential phase.

He evolved a tasting menu of combining elements that would offer discerning clients more choice and freedom of expression; it was an instant success, especially among reviewers, who appreciated its interactive qualities. The new *menu dégustation* at NoFood was mentioned gratefully in many food columns. Hardy felt he had found his feet at last with the tasting menu and quite looked forward to going over it all again comfortably with Carl, with whom he had a tradition of late-night snacking. His headwaiter had a refined palate for all his vagueness and was an excellent dining companion who paid genuine attention to business. His extreme beauty and blankness were disconcerting—Hardy often had the feeling that he was at a child's tea party with a doll and had to repress the urge to rearrange him in his chair—but he had learned to work around this.

On his first day back, Hardy caught Carl shooting up in the kitchen. "What?" he said, scandalized. "You know I don't allow drugs on the premises, Carl. Unless this is related to your rehabilitation," he added as an afterthought, trying to picture carrying on the farce of NoFood without him.

"Not drugs," said Carl briefly, rolling down his sleeve, "micronutrients."

"Is this some weird vitamin thing? Painkillers? Can't you just take pills?"

"No way to digest them anymore. I've had a bypass. Total gastric bypass. I'll never need to eat again. Just have to take a batch of nutrients from time to time. No shitting. No disease. Clean inside and out."

"Carl, what do you mean? Everybody needs to eat."

"Not any more. Not me. They've cleaned all my guts out, whole digestive tract, gone; I decided to get in on the first generation. Apparently the surgery isn't likely to change that much, and you can always update your nutrients as they come along."

"They cut your guts out?" whispered Hardy, unable to believe what he was hearing. He heaved suddenly and threw up his morning coffee all over the floor.

"Yeah," said Carl, guiding him to a chair and finding a mop, "I'll never have to do that again." He gestured to the splatter on the tiles. "I can still eat if I want to, but I don't have to."

"But where does the food go?" asked Hardy, repelled.

"Frictionless bioflex tubing. Passes all the way through. Gravity feed and some sphincter action."

"Carl, that is disgusting. The most disgusting thing I've heard in my life. You volunteered for this? Were you sick?"

"Nah, it's elective. I just don't want to get sick. Ever. My father died of colon cancer."

"So now your insides are full of coils of plastic and you can never eat again?"

"Yes."

"You're crazy."

"Soon everyone will be doing it. You'll see. TGB. It's the next big thing."

Carl was right. TGB took the world of lifestyle surgery by storm. Within a few months TGB clinics were booked solid for years ahead, even harder to get into than Arar's restaurant, and that restaurant had obtained a whole new lease on life. Where there is no need to eat, there is no need to serve food, yet neither obviates the need to dine out.

Hardy found himself accidentally in possession of the formula for the unkillable restaurant. The only fallible link in the chain was him, the determinedly ageing icon. Otherwise NoFood could go on purveying ineffable food to the impermeable interiors of its ageless clientele forever. Yet he knew that it was the Arar cult of personality that kept the restaurant afloat. All he had to do was give in, acknowledge the absurdity of being a chef, and walk away. NoFood would fold overnight. But he would not give in.

He could not give in. He had no idea how. He had to be a chef, and had known it since he was ten years old. Cooking was how he related to the world. There are things to eat; there are processes of making them edible and pleasurable; there are people to eat them. Otherwise it was all incomprehensible.

He found, though, as time went on, that he was relieved that his food, which he prepared with his own hands, was not passing through the miles of hospital tubing sitting around him on the uncomfortable chairs. The no-food concept insulated him from the horrors of TGB. He told himself continuously: he was feeding people's minds. He worked away assiduously at menu development, creating an army of imaginary dishes that he could keep between himself and his gutted clientele.

He had no more of his three a.m. feasts with Carl, even though Carl seemed perfectly willing to continue them. He even seemed disappointed, though it was hard to tell. But

Hardy could not bear to see his canapés disappearing into the plastic void of his maw. It made him gag.

He lived the life of a culinary hermit for seven years. He loved his restaurant and had no intention of quitting it—in fact, he rarely left it, he had dragged the office futon out to the middle of the floor in the deserted kitchen—but he found he was no longer comfortable amongst his patrons. He had used to take proprietary strolls through the crowded room on a regular basis—severe, skinny, and regal with his shambling strides—but now he couldn't. He could take no pleasure in doling out his small, stiff nods.

He was not serving his TGB patrons any food, and it would not do them any good if he did. He could not help them.

Suddenly his own digestion seemed the most precious thing in the world. He had always been prone to hyperacidity. Now every burp and cramp was cherished. Going to the bathroom, always a ceremonious event, became something worthy of serious dramaturgy. Every time he sat down on the toilet he thought of Carl, disemboweled, floating emptily about the world like a soap bubble. What did he do with all the time he now had? You can only do so much yoga.

His sleep was rocky. The determination of everybody else to stop eating had made him stop sleeping, or just about. He was like a pilot study for a technique of sleep removal. As he stared glassy-eyed at the hanging copper pans in the kitchen from his futon for the seventh or eighth straight hour each night, he wondered if he should turn himself in to the nearest hospital; no doubt there was some feature of his brain chemistry that could contribute to the next major revision of the human animal.

From this somnambulistic fog he awoke one night at the restaurant: the night of Seychelles' eighteenth birthday. He had been slowly upping the ante on the no-food experience, freeing up more and more choice on the menus, now typically presenting a list of elementary ingredients for appetizers, for mains, for desserts, that people could combine at will.

These combined orders he would rate from his kitchen seclusion—Carl brought them to him—according to a precise but unexplainable personal scale, based on the ideal dishes he had imagined for the evening.

Hardy was fishing.

Having reached nearly rock bottom, his scorekeeping was a means of reaching out, monitoring for a kindred soul. People failed him continually. One evening, impressed with a particular appetizer, he had sent Carl out to the front with a blank restaurant card: "tell them to order anything" he said, and waited. Nothing came of it, despite his anticipation: the wished-for dish was humdrum. This happened twice more. The fourth time, though, a simple, lovely salad that he had not even thought of himself came through the door in Carl's magnificent cursive: Seychelles' order.

"Who is it?" he rasped out to Carl, his heart quickening.

"I don't know her," said Carl. "Young girl, pretty, smart. Here with two friends, looks like an occasion. They're playing it cool. Booked two years ago. My bet is a birthday."

"Right," said Hardy, dryly. "Break out the cake." He handed three blank white cards to the waiter.

"Do you think she'll know what to do with it?"

"We'll see," said Hardy.

She did. Her friends' orders were forgettable—though not forgotten, he saved them, instinctively registering their importance, instead of throwing them out with the contempt they would otherwise have deserved—but Seychelles' was unprecedented. Carl said she was still a teenager. She was almost certainly TGB, probably hadn't eaten for years, still in the initial euphoria. What she would know about the real taste of braised short ribs with yellow mash was debatable; who cooked real meat now, especially beef, such a hassle compared to synthetics, and half the time listed for viral scares? It was highly unlikely she would ever have had such a dish; it took half a day to prepare and needed real conductive heat and metal pans.

Yet somehow she had thought of it, in its simplicity and perfection. Maybe she had eaten beef before, once. Or something. Hardy was electrified. He hardly dared to leave his kitchen sanctum. He crept out to see her as if she were a specimen of a rare flower or an extinct species, last holdout of some tiny, precious biosphere. The girl who could taste his food. Could it be?

"She said," explained Carl with a glint in his eye, "—about her order—she said it was slow but she could afford to wait."

"Really?" said Hardy, in the grip of some indefinable emotion, perhaps fear of impending happiness, putting on a fresh set of whites. She could afford to wait? How long had he been waiting, now?

He went out into his restaurant for the first time in years to meet Seychelles, the ridiculously young, the stupefyingly rich Seychelles, TGB princess. He met her; she agreed to eat his food. She came back the next night—he closed the restaurant, without warning or explanation, in sheer Arar caprice—and ate the ribs he had spent all day cooking, riven by inner dissensions.

She loved them.

He could tell that she did, even though she was wasted on her inhaled medication, trying to be blasé while dining with the great chef. Arar had found his muse. Washing the dishes afterward—actual plates with gravy on them, he thought about framing them instead—he remembered her spontaneous laugh as she had pushed his hand down into the water of that damn fool Lucite table. Somehow she had found the fun in that piece of preciousness. He decided to let the Lucite tables remain in the restaurant for another week. Their designer was overjoyed, got a full page spread in a major magazine, and won a design award.

Seychelles seemed so real to him, so innocent, so complete, that he could almost ignore her being TGB. He was so bound up in the cooking that he did not at first perceive that a courtship was what he was getting into.

43

Seychelles quickly got over her awe of Arar because she liked his food so much. The food talked. Hardy was taciturn. It took her a while to truly understand the quality of what she got, but she learned to appreciate his eloquence, and he watched her blossom into a connoisseur. So their courtship was indeed slow, just like those braised ribs she had first ordered.

At first, Seychelles offered to pay for the wonderful meals he was cooking for her. After all, she could have bought No-Food a hundred times over.

"What?' said Hardy, "No, of course not! You are my guest. And NoFood is no longer in the business of serving real food. This is something else."

"What, then?"

Hardy had no immediate answer to this. Gradually, though, he began to cook for people she knew. For her parents. He found himself being dragged around to the hot spots, spending futile hours at checkpoints, trying to entertain the various animated haircuts that she called her friends. He was continuously appalled at what people ate, or failed to eat, on these occasions, however, and tried to keep them to a minimum. He still found being surrounded by the TGB unnerving.

He was willing and able, though, to have sex with the beautiful and surgically optimized Seychelles, even though she was TGB, as he discovered upon trial. It was okay to grasp her body from the outside, much less intimate than worrying about what went on once food had disappeared inside her.

He also enjoyed the company of her parents. He found them restful. They were so blindingly rich as to have lost sight of basic distinctions: they lived on an astral plane entirely without negatives and consequently were unable to recognize them. Even fundamental laws, such as gravity, were often suspended in their presence. Thus there was very little bickering.

Additionally, Seychelles' father Magellan was not yet TGB. This was unusual in a man so rich, but he had taken awhile to make up his mind, and had secured OR spaces for his wife Silvia and his daughter first, anyway. "First selfless, then gutless," he quipped. Hardy winced. But in general they got on very well.

Hardy even had hopes that he might remain unfashionably natural and tried, rather clumsily, to persuade him— "think, man, about the food you'd be throwing away! Only three people in the world can get it—"

It was not to be. A year into his relationship with Seychelles, her parents booked a theatre trip to Santa Monica— her father had an eccentric passion for the stage, and live actors, that her mother had long had to put up with, unfashionable though it was—to celebrate his imminent surgery. Just a little getaway, they had said. Last chance to exercise that gut feeling, said Magellan.

A crazed critic got past the security checkpoint with a rare isotope that killed the entire cast and the audience. Magellan, not yet TGB, was the first to die of radiation poisoning. His wife lasted a little longer. Amazingly, she had not blamed him, or at least never in Hardy's hearing. Somehow their serenity lasted to the end. Perhaps they had simply never learned how to argue, having no need for it.

Hardy, whose guts clenched every time he saw them on the monitor, held Seychelles' freezing cold hand and navigated Magellan's last few jokes. Live theatre? More like dead theatre. Who can kill a hologram, eh?

Silvia sat next to him, watching him admiringly, pityingly. She said nothing. The most emotional person they talked to from the sanatorium was Fortescue, their friend who owned the theatre, who was dying in the next ward. He was tearfully apologetic. A theatre man to the end, he hanged himself expertly in the foyer and left a long manifesto.

Hardy and Seychelles were married in her palatial house in front of the monitor—and a JP, though he was incidental to the proceedings. He muttered a few forgettable words, and so did they, but chiefly the event was about Seychelles wearing the starkly simple gown she had designed, and her mother's tiara, in her parents' sight as they sat, looking blue and faded, radioactive, in faraway California. Both wept for the only time as they saw their daughter in their own drawing room, standing formally in front of the mantel decorated with flowers. She was a glorious bride.

Their private wedding feast was spectacular, and memorable in that it was one of only a handful of occasions in Hardy's career on which he was willing to overlook embargo: it turned out that lobsters, exceedingly rare, were re-listed that day. Hardy pretended to himself that he had not received the lawyer's update and cooked them anyway as a gesture of commitment to Seychelles. He did not tell her about it, though. He just gave her the lobsters, perfectly steamed, with brown butter.

He soon found himself cooking many of the consolatory meals he had made for himself after his parents had died: rich and strange, they were full of odd combinations that surprised him after so many years. He hadn't written them down. They just came back to him.

He would walk into the kitchen and find Seychelles in tears, rummaging through the cupboards. "Oh sweetheart," he would say, taking her shoulders, sitting her down, making tea. Then he would start rummaging through the cupboards himself, making some dish he hadn't thought of for twenty years. It was like automatic writing. He would narrate the twists and turns of the recipes as he went, as Seychelles gradually ceased sniffling in the background: "I made this on the day of my parents' funeral. I think you would have liked them, Seychelles. They loved food."

"They loved you, Hardy."

"Yes, that too. I remember: I was using up the last of the ingredients I had bought at Fiasco's on the day they were killed. It was a weird list, but it was all I had left. Everything in the house was destroyed. Nori. God, who cooks with nori now, after the Pacific thing? Well, we'll use this dulse. Atlantic. Tricky to work with, thinner, but then, I guess you never had real nori, did you?"

"No."

"Dried tomatoes, purple, grown somewhere way out west where they still grow them in the ground. I remember Fichu at the store saying you could still taste the earth in them. And what would that taste like, Fichu? I said, but he was always getting me with lines like that. He was a salesman."

"Yes, I think I met him once right after we were married."

"Well, it was an unpropitious combination. And chicken stock, fresh frozen. This was before they had stabilized the gene pool again. It was really hard to come by. Most of those generations had practically no bones. Lousy stock."

"So that's why the freezer looks like a mass grave, is it?"

"These things are hard to get over. I had to hoard bones for a long time—like a beagle. Honestly! Anyway, I had bought a lot of stock. I had to rush it across town: it was melting. I remember: I left it at Felipe's while I made the arrangements. He had no freezer. Disaster. To make a long story short, I had to make soup. What else was there to do, I ask you?"

"Soup is traditional comfort food."

"Because it's supposed to re-hydrate you after you've been weeping, Seychelles, my love. I guess it worked that way for me. You?"

"It's still comfort food, Hardy."

"Okay then.'

"Okay."

They ate soup. It was decent, considering.

Their nuptial bliss was interrupted three years later by the debilitating struggle over children. Seychelles wanted to go ahead with having a child, and so did Hardy, until he realized that Seychelles was no longer in possession of her uterus and intended to farm it out. He endured endless lectures on the dangers of uterine and ovarian cancer and tried to reconcile himself to this reproductive method. But whole sections of his personality, including his sex drive, would freeze up at the very thought of it.

He spent a lot of time throwing up at the restaurant, being comforted by Carl with tea and cold compresses. It was an awful period. "Carl," he said, in his desperation to confront his own fears. "How did you do it?"

"Do what?" said Carl, imperturbably.

"What do you mean, what? Go to the doctors and let them cut your guts out, of course! How can you live that way?"

"What do you mean, Hardy?"

"What do I mean? I mean that my wife cannot carry my child! That she's over, she's stuck, she's closed, nothing can grow in her, it's all gone! We love each other, and there's nothing we can do about it!"

"Hardy, that's not true. Your genetic material is still in your balls, just fine, and Seychelles' is in the bank. All you need to do is agree, and she can make it happen."

"She can make it happen? Carl, that's disgusting! You mean, like ordering out? No! I can't…"

"Hardy," said Carl, with his zen finality, "what can I say? You and Seychelles will have written the recipe. What does it matter who cooks it?"

"Jesus, Carl, how can you say that? Do you have any children?"

"No," said Carl.

"Then how can you say that?"

"Look," said Carl. "You and Seychelles want a baby, right?"

"Yes," said Hardy.

"And you're proud to have invented all those dishes at NoFood?"

"Yes," said Hardy.

"Why can't you see it's the same thing? Yes, some other woman will grow the baby, she'll spend her energy on it, feed it—this is precious, it's important, I know, but it's not everything, I dunno; she's the home cook—"

"Carl!"

"Hardy!" said Carl, with unusual energy: "Shut up! Listen to Seychelles! She's the one who had her guts out, not you. Don't you see how important that is? She's tried to save herself, to improve her odds. To live with you, and the world she loves, longer. She's extended her own life, and not prejudiced her children's. She can still do it. Let her! What's it gonna cost you?"

Hardy could not do it. Seychelles walked out on him, and he could not blame her, though he tried to. The only good thing to come out of it was that it made him close NoFood. By then, the restaurant was a millstone. In his despair he summarily shut it down. He put the indefatigable Carl on a retainer and randomly, immediately, took the first outcountry flight available, which was to Taipei. He had heard that the city had some of the finest restaurants left in the blasted Asias.

There were some good restaurants in Taipei, and in one of them he contracted a local immunovirus. This cut short his culinary visit, though he had not been appreciating things as he would otherwise have done—there was little or no TGB in evidence, for example—due to his condition of stunned misery. He spent eight months deathly ill in a hospital there, receiving the best care on Seychelles' medical annuity, feeling as if he had been struck down by the gods. The doctors told him he had a virus; they knew its name and properties. As far as he was concerned he was sick from guilt and thwarted love. A chance form from the insurers, signed by Seychelles in her tight backward-slant printing, drove him back home and into a reconciliation. He went to therapy. He tried and tried again for a sperm donation, but it never happened.

After this, grimly childless, they jointly decided not to reopen NoFood. All the domestic cooking, dinner parties, and charity functions had given Hardy an idea: the idea that was to become Floating Island, the most elite of all supper clubs, their next enterprise. Seychelles helped him out with practical development, and so did Donovan, their embargo lawyer and Seychelles' longtime friend. She offered to host their first catered event at her spectacular apartment, with her even more spectacular client list. So Floating Island roared into being, and never let up.

Hardy now desperately desired real food—just to handle plain fruits and vegetables and meat. He was determined to make all the dishes he had only made up at NoFood. At the same time he could not stand another series of total misunderstandings of his mission. Newly protected by the cordon of Seychelles' wealth, he opened a private club, even more understated than his restaurant had been.

Floating Island was their baby, the operation that they devised together and ran together. It stabilized at about forty members, enough to keep them as busy as they wanted to be. The club became a secret success, an urban legend, with no press releases or information about members or venues, constantly speculated about in gossip columns and spitefully mourned in food magazines: reason for the disappearance of Arar from the public eye.

Hardy's menus, which had started out baroque with his pent-up feelings, gradually simplified toward a more natural, pristine style. Seychelles helped more and more in the kitchen as well as with the organizational side. Everything grew more integrated. Arar looked back over his ambitious career from time to time and was surprised to find himself the proprietor of a supper club. Yet he felt he had not come down but grown up.

"Weird, isn't it," he said to Seychelles, "that I only feel like I've arrived now that we're running a peripatetic restaurant?"

"Life is a work in progress, Hardy," she replied.

He was happy. He found he didn't even much mind being surrounded by the TGBers when he was working in their houses. The domestic environment, more diffuse and distracting than the professionalism of a restaurant kitchen, kept his anxieties at bay: people seemed more whole at home. Diners only ever bring parts of themselves to a restaurant, and there was something about this that made their TGB more evident; all the aspects of their personalities that they had excised to become their restaurant selves always brought their mutilated innards hideously to the fore in Hardy's mind. Such people were a lot less creepy standing in their own kitchens and eating at their own tables.

He looked out over the bent heads of the dining company one day, twelve guests in all, at Donovan's elegant, stratospheric, all-glass penthouse and was reminded—certainly not by the décor—of the banqueting table that he had despised at Cakes and Ale. What was absurdity then was camaraderie now. From the head of the table, he beamed at the collected diners who were talking quietly, nodding, chewing, cutlery and stemware clinking, not raucous but attentive, devoted; he beamed fondly at the memory of his severe twenty-year-old self. Seychelles gazed at him across the length of the table and threw him a dazzling smile.

Five months later Hardy was dead. It turned out that his hyperacidity of late was stomach cancer. The irony of this was not lost on him. It was already inoperable, so at least he was spared the final assault on his identity that yielding to surgery—or even to TGB itself—would have represented. "I get to go out naturally," he said to Seychelles with dignity, "like I came in. All parts present and correct."

This was neither tactful nor true, as his ulcerated guts were surely no longer correct, but no one expects either tact or accuracy from the dying. Seychelles did not, at least. She ate up everything he had to say; she ate up every crumb of food he offered; in the wildness of her grief after his death she considered eating him up, full stop, but settled for preserving him like a finely-cured ham.

Hardy kept cooking till very late in the game. He and Seychelles cooked and ate all their favorite meals together, high spots from twenty-two years dedicated to food, until he collapsed in the kitchen one day and gave himself a third-degree burn. Thereafter he reclined in a chair attached to various machines, and she did the cooking. When this became too frustrating—there is nothing worse to have in your kitchen than a disabled chef—he waited quietly in his room in the hospital suite for her to bring the food to him. He was gracious about it when it arrived.

He was gracious to the end, Hardwicke Arar. He was satisfied. He was still in possession of his nose; he was still in possession of his principles; he was still in possession of his own digestive tract. He had cooked the best food in the world, real and imaginary, and found someone to eat it.

"Seychelles, my love," he said, finally: "it's late. It's a long walk to the kitchen. Go make yourself some tea. Make it properly."

They discussed what kind of tea to make and settled on orange blossom, an old favorite. When she came back, the cup in her hands was warm. Hardy was not.

Crystalline Donuts

It is hard to think of an object less crystalline than a donut. They do not have a lattice structure. They have no known refractive indices. Nonetheless, that was the name of Fats Bester's donut shop: Crystalline Donuts. It expressed to him the superbness of the donut form. In addition to the nearly infinite variety of doughs, fillings, and toppings, there was the shape: there was something profoundly satisfying about the shape of a donut.

It was the hole in the middle that did it. The idea of selling to a customer—along with his food, or her food—a half-centimeter of air was compelling. It was a giddy thing to contemplate, to be a merchant of air, the stuff of life. Water, of course, was a hotly contested commodity, priceless everywhere, but even the most determined capitalists had not yet got round to selling air, except in space. Needless to say, Fats sold only round donuts at the shop—round with a hole. He was a purist. No twists. No stupid little balls. No cakes, muffins, bagels, crumpets, biscotti, or any other donut wannabes.

There was also the matter of frying. It is a truth universally acknowledged, if we are being honest with ourselves, that fried food is best. Real donuts are fried. Herein lies the uniqueness of donuts: dough that is not baked, but fried. Not wimpily shallow-fried, but fried with real commitment, in lovely bubbling vats. Fats used canola oil by preference, though it was hard to get. Half the earth was covered with rapeseed, it seemed—the new strains were practically unkillable and spread like wildfire—but it wasn't used for food much. Critical industries took it all. There is nothing more critical than eating, but this fact had escaped whatever authorities made these decisions. So Fats was forced to fall back on combinations of palm and cottonseed and corn oil on a regular basis, or whatever else was going. In the powerful international market for vegetable grease, the claims of donut fryers rated low. It was a constant sorrow to him.

The shop was in a decent part of town. It was safe. It was near transit. Toxicity levels were fairly low. He had paid through the nose for good filtration, so he could just stay in during the never-ending smog alerts instead of wasting all that time at evac stations. There was no telling what you might come home to when you went to one of those places; smog and crime went hand in hand. It was impossible to run a business if you were away two days out of three, anyway. His profit margins were not fabulous, and it took him a long time to pay the system off, but he could never have gotten ahead without it. Also, he found, as a bonus, that the exchange unit really pumped out donut smell when he was frying. The place smelled delicious as you came toward it on the street, and there was no doubt that it enhanced his trade. Sometimes he even had lineups.

He divided his donuts into three types: light—which referred to texture, not calories, about which he did not concern himself—old-fashioned, and flavored. His least favorite were the light ones, though he prided himself on his mastery of the form. They were white and pillowy, a high aerated dough, golden crust, his most popular sellers. Privately he called them "marshmallows." He was an old-fashioned man. He liked the denser, crumby texture, the shock combination of vanilla and fat, the deep-fried look, and above all the narrow and elegant form of old-fashioned donuts: the "big o" as he called it. Lots of air for sale there. In terms of flavored, he offered a changing roster of both kinds, light and old-fashioned, according to whim and availability, a lot of which had to do with embargo status. Many of his flavorings were imported—rose water, for example, a personal invention of his, terrific in the old-fashioned dough—and were always going up and down on the admit lists. He didn't make a big deal about it and stockpiled when he could. He bought chocolate whenever he could find it, at whatever price. It was more precious than gold.

He lived alone above the shop in a nice apartment. His first wife, his high school sweetheart—also a donut fan—had died of asthma. His second had developed an allergy to canola oil. He had valiantly switched over to palm olein, had the whole place professionally cleaned, changed over all his recipes, but she left him anyway. She could sense his reluctance to leave the premises, and he had become associated in her mind with suffering. He was also getting fat.

After her departure, he continued to do so. So, Fats was fat. There was no doubt about it. Donuts were his passion and consolation. He went on tinkering with cardamom and extract of mint—so suitable to the cool, cloudy puffiness of the "marshmallows"—and orange essence, and got fatter and fatter.

One morning a divinity walked in the door. He was blond and perfected and seemed to be surrounded by a nimbus of light; for the first time the donuts may actually have looked crystalline in his glory. Fats was stunned. He forgot to release the button he was pressing on the coffee machine—not that it was real coffee, of course—and scalded his finger. The thrill of pain brought tears to his eyes and enhanced the general misty effect of his customer.

"Hi," said this vision, "—the coffee, watch it. Oops. Sorry."

"Can I help you?" gasped Fats, shaking his burnt finger and feeling that there were likely to be few areas in which this man needed his help. Unless he needed a donut, of course. Fats regained his self-command and ran his finger under the cold tap.

"Is it real coffee?" asked the man.

"No."

"No thanks on that, then. But I would like a donut."

"You drink real coffee?" asked Fats.

"Yes. When I do."

"I didn't think there was any left."

"There's very little. Sometimes my employer gets it."

"Who's that?"

"I work at a restaurant. His name is Hardwicke Arar. The chef?"

This name meant nothing to Fats, though clearly it was significant. He felt the dawnings of kinship with this celestial being: they were both in food service.

"What would you say is your favorite?" asked the man, gesturing to the neat rows before him under glass.

"Me? For me, it's old-fashioned every time. They're more substantial. Plain, usually, though I will put in a good word for the double cardamoms."

"You make them in-house?"

"In-house. Yes," replied Fats, proudly.

"Right," said the man. "One plain and one double cardamom, and a cup of black tea."

"Good choice," said Fats, putting them into a bag and handing over a flex cup of steaming tea. The man went to the window where he could see the street, chose one of Fat's four tables, and sat down. He did not read the monitor, or any paper, or wear earphones of any kind. He sat, looked out of the window, and ate both donuts quietly. Sometimes he even gazed at them as they went from his hand to his mouth. Fats saw people staring open-mouthed at him through the glass, but whether it was because of his extreme beauty or this unusual behavior he could not tell. When the man was done, he came back to the counter.

"Those were excellent donuts," he said, "the best I've ever had. Thank you."

"You're welcome," said Fats automatically, trying to focus on the man's impossibly handsome face, his bristling silvery hair and perfect eyebrows, though his glance kept sliding off his cheekbones out into the glowing air around him. He could not recall ever having been thanked in the shop before. All in all, he thought he would remember it as a unique experience.

But it proved not to be unique. Thereafter, the extraordinarily gorgeous man dropped in from time to time, perhaps twice a week. Serially and precisely, he tried all the different kinds of donut, always ordering one plain old-fashioned as a kind of anchor. Fats, who did this himself, recognized the signs of a connoisseur. The man always came in the morning.

"I have to be at the restaurant by two," he explained politely.

"What restaurant is it?" asked Fats, who had been wanting to ask this for a while.

"NoFood."

"You work at NoFood?" Fats had heard of NoFood; it was the most famous restaurant on the planet. "Isn't that the place that doesn't serve any food?"

"Yes," said the man crisply.

"What do you do, then?"

"I'm the headwaiter."

"But what do you *do*?"

"I wait tables. I bring people the menu and take down their orders, bring their bills. I manage a staff of twelve."

"People pay to sit there and not eat anything? What do they do?"

"They talk. They pose for the cameras getting out of the helicopter. They make deals and meet their publicists. They congratulate themselves on getting a reservation."

"Amazing," said Fats, at a loss for anything else to say. Then he blurted: "But don't you think it's a terrible idea?"

"Yes," said the headwaiter with gravity.

"Don't you like food? You like donuts!"

"Yes," he replied seriously, "I like food. Donuts, certainly. I wouldn't do what I do for anyone else but Arar. It is a terrible idea. Tragic, like an old Greek play. Arar was driven to it. No one took his perfect food—he is to high cuisine what you are to donuts—seriously. They ignored it. He couldn't stand it, so he took it away from them."

"And they kept coming?"

"Yes. Nobody was more surprised than he. He wanted to drive them away, all those customers who came to the restaurant and talked and didn't even notice the food." Fats thought grimly of all the lovingly made donuts he had sold to people who ate them while driving or talking on the phone, who vaguely noticed that they were sweet, but that was all.

"Were you surprised?"

"No. I figured they would keep coming till the world ends. Or till Arar quits, whichever comes first."

"Wow. How long have you been working for him?"

"Since he opened NoFood: fifteen years. What about you—how long have you been running this place?"

"Fourteen years. Well, this is the fifteenth."

"And what is your name, Mr Donut?" Fats had been wondering how to ask this himself; in that awkward way of over-the-counter conversations, they had gone past the point at which it could be asked naturally.

"Fats Bester," he said with relief, extending his hand, "yours?"

"Carl Cutworth." They shook hands. "I was wondering—" He hesitated politely.

"Yes?"

"—about these signs." He gestured minimally—you could not quite say he pointed—with his manicured hands to the printed cards identifying each rack of donuts under the glass counter. Fats printed them out because his handwriting was awful. The point had always annoyed him, actually, because he felt that his donuts had an artisanal quality that would be better expressed by dashing handwritten signs. Both his wives had had round, girly writing that was not appropriate either. Carl continued with a modesty that seemed genuine, "Well, I do calligraphy. Not at all fancy. Very plain. I handwrite all the orders and menus at the restaurant. I thought you might want a few signs. Your donuts deserve them. Just a touch of class, without overdoing it, you know."

"Really? Terrific, I say. I tried doing my own but they were ridiculous. Do you need special paper?"

"I'll bring some next time."

"Well, thanks. Thanks a lot. I look forward to it."

"No problem," said Carl. He came back two days later with some perfect white cards that looked like they had been cut to order. He sat down at a table, took a silver pen out of his pocket, and wrote on each of them, rapidly, unfussily — "old-fashioned," "light," "flavored." They were elegant, masculine, uncompromising. He then did an extra series in consultation with Fats: "chocolate," "double cardamom," "rose" (nice, said Carl, haven't tried those), "mint," "orange."

That day the donuts were on the house. Fats offered him a dozen to go: "no," said Carl seriously, "I prefer to eat them here." Fats was doubly gratified, and the new signs subtly transformed the whole room. He spent the afternoon sitting out front where he could admire them. They were exactly right, expressing the handmade seriousness of his donuts without being grandmotherly and doilyish.

Carl became one of the most regular of his regulars. Every now and again he renewed the signs if they yellowed with grease. One day, in the most calm and unassuming way, he said "let me show you something" and made a minute adjustment to the spacing of the tables. He moved them about eight inches all told but the difference was incredible. He had jogged them just out of their previous symmetry, and the room looked about twice as large. Somehow it appeared as if there were fewer tables, but there were still four. Fats was impressed. The guy was a professional. "I thought they would look better," said Carl.

Fats sat in his new palatial, authoritative donut shop when Carl was not there and wondered if he was falling victim to a decorator. What would he do if Carl showed up with flowers? What would he do if he liked them? But Carl did no more interfering. He was content just to sit there and eat Fats' donuts, looking like a visiting god. A series of young women, and sometimes men, tended to show up predictably on mornings when Carl was around. He smiled at them distantly but did not encourage them. It was primarily the donuts he was interested in, and secondarily Fats, who made them.

One day Fats asked him, rather randomly, how he stayed so slim. Of the many perfections of Carl, this was not necessarily the most noticeable, but it was of obvious and explicable interest to Fats, and therefore seemed harmless.

"Ah," said Carl, betraying no surprise. "I'm TGB."

Fats looked blank for a moment. Then it came to him. It was rare in his circle. As far as he knew, he'd never met one before. "Is that where—?"

"They cut your guts out? Yeah. Total gastric bypass."

"But you can still eat?"

"Yes. I don't have to, but I like to. It feels more normal."

"But you could go forever, not eating?"

"Yes."

"Why did you do it? If you don't mind my asking."

"Not just to stay slim, you mean? Well, for health on the one side: cuts down the risks. My dad died of bowel disease."

"Oh, I'm sorry," said Fats hastily.

"No, it was a long time ago now. But I love surgery."

"You do?" Fats quailed at doctors.

"Yes, I can't help it. I want to be new all the time. Always changing. People think it's vanity, but it's not: it's the desire to be different, to keep moving. It's the human condition, at least as I see it."

Fats glanced anxiously down at his belly, suddenly seeing it as a sign of stagnation: not the human condition? But then, most humans he knew had their own bowels. And plenty in his life had changed over the past fifteen years as his fat had grown: there, see, it was change, too. Natural change. For a fleeting moment he looked at the impeccable Carl with a twinge of superiority.

He felt considerably less superior after his checkup two days layer. He had been type 2 for a while, and let's face it, what exactly is the point of exercising for hours every day and eating whole wheat bread if you're also, inevitably, going to eat donuts? There was no way he was going to control his diabetes by diet, or lifestyle, or any of those other words meaningless to most people. Well, now he was going on insulin. He had been expecting it, but it was still a shock, and having to give himself needles was harrowing.

He found that his fear of doctors extended even toward playing doctor on himself. Before every injection a sweaty debate occurred between voices in his head: one the shrieky voice of a terrified five-year-old, and the other a horrible, false-hearty family-practice voice that he must have subliminally remembered from childhood. It certainly sounded nothing like the lifeless near-whisper of his current doctor. That dry little voice had more and more to say as the months wore on, and none of it was good. Fats, who had probably been diabetic even before he was fat, but never knew it because he felt fine, or what he thought was fine, now began to feel bad.

He tried to regulate his life: ate at alarm-clock precise times; tried to walk more, as the dry voice advised, though this is nearly impossible when you can hardly go outside because of poisoned air. He just couldn't give up donuts; they were intrinsic to his being. It was hard enough cutting out the spontaneity of them—this is the point, after all, of snack food—and fitting them in to his timed, calorie-counted meals. He ate no other sweets. He drank no alcohol. But he was damned if he was going to cut them out altogether. There would be nothing to live for.

Fats got less fat, but he looked no better. In fact, he looked worse. He got dark circles under his eyes. His feet swelled. His doctor kept sending him to specialists, many of whose specialties he'd never even heard of before and none of whom he could afford, really. In a burst of paranoia after Angie's death he had taken out insurance and had kept paying it pro forma all these years; he had enough coverage to get by like this for a while, one referral a week, but sooner or later he would hit a wall. Some red flag would go up; they would start refusing his ever-changing claims. The problem with diabetes is that it is always becoming something else.

Carl had been looking concerned about him for some time. Fats was looking haggard, feeling rotten, working half days—which could not go on—and had given up on flavored.

All he was selling these days were light and straight old-fashioned. Carl obviously interpreted this as serious. In his implacably direct way, one day, seeing Fats sitting exhaustedly on his stool behind the counter covered in a cold sweat, he came out with the proposal: "Look Fats, I think you should consider TGB."

Fats was floored. That is, he kept sitting there clutching his stool and leaning his hot back against the cold wall—if he had tried to stand up, he would have been floored, and been wholly unable to get up again. So he stayed where he was and regarded Carl with amazement. So many objections rushed into his mind at once he was unable to work out their priority, and it took him a moment to start speaking.

"Carl," he began, "you must be crazy. I couldn't afford it in a million years. Not to mention that I have no intention of giving my guts away. Plus, who says it would help, anyway?"

"Is it diabetes?" asked Carl.

"Yes."

"Then it will help. It should solve it entirely. It is one of the diseases it was designed to combat."

"Really? Then why hasn't my doctor mentioned it?"

"He probably assumes you can't afford it. Who's your insurer?"

"Intramural something."

"Only a few of the top-end ones will cover it. Otherwise it's considered elective."

"Well, that rules me right out then. If I would even consider such a thing. Which I wouldn't."

"I know it sounds extreme. But it will take care of it absolutely. Permanently. You ask your practitioner and see. You'll just need nutrients with adiponectin and you'll be fine. Slim, too, of course." Carl smiled. "I can pay for it."

"What?"

"I can pay for it," repeated Carl.

"Carl! That's insane! Why? How?"

"I have a deal with my surgeon. If I recommend clients to him, he will do work for free. So I'd be helping myself as well as you."

"Carl, you're nuts. Buy-one-get-one-free operations?"

"Yes. I have a lot of coverage; it won't cost me that much. You talk to your doctor and ask about this guy; he's famous. I'll give you his card."

"Carl," said Fats weakly, feeling unreal and not sure what he was agreeing to as he took the card from Carl's hand, "this is weird. I don't think I should let you do something like this for me."

"Don't worry about it. I'd like to do it. Who else makes donuts like you? I'd be doing the world a favor." Fats' grey cheeks pinkened. It was so rare anyone gave donuts the respect they deserved.

"But—"

"I'm a lot older than I look, Fats. I have no family. Let me do this for you."

Fats took the card to his doctor, who was overjoyed, so overjoyed he actually raised his voice. "Mr Bester!" he practically shouted, pumping Fats' hand, "I congratulate you! Even to get an appointment with this man is more than I can do! He is the foremost TGB surgeon in town—which is to say, anywhere. His clinic is booked to infinity, but if this friend can secure you a preliminary appointment, maybe he can somehow get you OR space as well. Time is of the essence in this case, Mr Bester—maybe this argument will carry some weight with him, as most of his clients will be lifestyle ones, no medical urgency…"

Time is of the essence? Oh dear, thought Fats.

He found himself hustled out the door into the hands of the secretary, who called the number on the card with every exhibition of awe, and got an appointment for the following week. She looked at Fats like he was a celebrity.

To his further amazement, Carl volunteered to go with him to the clinic. It was evident that he could tell that Fats needed moral support. Possibly his insight went so far as to intuit that Fats would not make it there at all without his help but would do a bunk at the last minute. Thus Carl, simply dressed as usual and, as usual, giving the impression that he reflected light, glided in on Tuesday morning to accompany him to Dr Olufsen's. He sat elegantly in the atrium of the hospital wing that Dr Olufsen commanded, surrounded by people of almost equal elegance, while Fats waddled tremulously in to consult with the great surgeon.

Olufsen was, if possible, more blindingly handsome than Carl, though not blond. He also exerted an air of preternatural calm. Fats wondered if there was something about the removal of the innards that contributed to self-possession—no stomach for churning? No spleen? Olufsen was clear about the benefits that TGB would offer Fats: "Your problem, Mr Bester, is primarily digestive. Remove the whole tract, remove the problem. The fact is that food is toxic to you. Your kidneys and liver are already failing; your heart is endangered, as is your whole circulatory system. Once we have stabilized you after the operation, you will find that your system is less strained with a reduction in blood volume, and your blood chemistry can be permanently and artificially stabilized with injectable nutrients with no interference from foods."

"I'll still have to take needles, huh?" asked Fats, focusing on facts he could take in.

"Yes, most likely," said Olufsen. "There are alternate medication methods for other drugs if necessary: transdermal patches, inhalers. Occasionally we install shunts for the nutrients in certain patients."

"What will happen to me if I don't have the operation?"

"I estimate you will be dead within a year," said the flawless doctor, gravely. This was a bit more direct than his own doctor, who tended to become elliptical when asked about Fats' prognosis.

"If you wish to schedule the preliminary trials with my clinician, please do so on the way out. The testing is thorough and takes two days; she can go over the procedures with you. As you are a recommendation of Carl's, should you wish to proceed, I can make a space in the clinic for you within three weeks upon your confirmation. Please let us know." He shook Fats' sweaty hand with glacial politeness and nodded him out the door. Fats went out feeling dazed. Carl stood up to meet him as he wandered into the atrium.

"What did he say?" asked Carl.

"He said I should come back for tests and that he can fit me in within three weeks," replied Fats promptly. Evidently some part of his brain had been listening for instructions, though it was not the part of which Fats was conscious. "And that I'll be dead within a year if I don't do it."

"That seems decisive."

"Does it?" asked Fats helplessly.

"I've had five surgeries with Olufsen, in addition to the TGB. He's the best in the business."

"Five more?"

"Yes," said Carl firmly. "I think you should go ahead, but it is up to you. At least go through the trials."

"Okay," said Fats.

"In that case, go to the secretary for the clinician. In here," said Carl, leading Fats like a blind man into an airy office.

"Right," said Fats. He spoke to the lady behind the desk, who looked at him pityingly because he was fat and distressed, and agreed to come back tomorrow, fasting, for the first series of pre-op tests. Carl saw him back to the shop and deposited him on his stool behind the counter. He turned in the doorway as he was leaving with the sympathetic reminder:

"No food after midnight, remember?" Fats nodded. Normally he hated fasting and always went in to his diabetic appointments starving and resentful. Now it seemed nothing—what was not eating from midnight to morning compared to not eating ever again?

The tests went fine; they were more thorough than anything Fats had undertaken before, and they revealed so much wrong with him that he was amazed he wasn't dead already. His state of disrepair was so dismal that he was shocked into acquiescence with the whole business. He signed up for the first available space.

He went through an interminable amount of paperwork with Carl: indemnity forms, insurer's forms, financial forms, statistics profile forms. Carl worked assiduously with his silver pen, documents spread out before him on Fats' table in the shop; some of the numbers on these forms were so high they were breathtaking. Carl was unperturbed by them. Seeing this, Fats finally let go of his guilt and accepted Carl's gift; it presented no hardship to him.

Two weeks later he was lying on a white bed in the gleaming hospital, staring fuzzily at Dr Olufsen and a horde of nurses and residents, ready for his total gastric bypass. He was too stoned to think of any last words, in the event he was about to die, so the white double doors with their round windows, portholes into the deluxe expanse of the operating theatre, hissed closed in silence.

Seventeen hours later he awoke in recovery, already feeling recovered. His sutured abdomen was decently covered with a light blanket. His belly lay a lot lower than before due to the preliminary liposuction they had conducted before opening, the nurse explained. If he ignored the various tubes coming out of his arms, he felt no worse than he did waking up on a typical morning. Anesthesia is a wonderful thing.

Even more wonderful, explained the recovery nurse, was the fact that they could keep pumping the painkillers into him throughout the healing process without fear of constipation and other digestive upsets: the first benefit of TGB. He would experience little or no pain—and no nausea—throughout his recovery. Recovery. The word dwelt in his euphoric brain. He was in recovery. Recovery. Strange word, made him feel like upholstery. But he had not so much been recovered as re-stuffed. Recovery. He drifted off again.

When he opened his eyes again Dr Olufsen was hovering there like a hologram advertising toothpaste or holidays. For a moment he thought it was Carl wearing a dark hat. "How are you feeling, Mr Bester?" he asked in his remote voice.

"Fine," said Fats, with a similar imperturbability. He seemed to be already catching on to the TGB emotionlessness, though it could be the tranquilizers. "Great."

"No pain?"

"Nope."

"You are responding well. We've been hydrating you—you'll have to do this periodically, preferably under medical supervision—and you have processed your first batch of nutrients normally. We may need to tweak them a bit to fit your system; every diabetic needs slightly different levels."

"I see," said Fats. "Am I allowed to eat?"

"Soon, but not yet. We need to allow some time for the flesh-to-flex connections to bond inside."

"Fine, fine," said Fats quickly. He did not want to hear about flesh-to-flex connections.

"The nurse will bring you some food at the appropriate time, in several days."

"Days?" said Fats, panicked.

"Yes," returned the doctor, "typically five days, though this will vary according to healing rates. Yours may be a little longer." Fats looked aghast. Dr Olufsen glanced at him with condescension, or compassion, or some emotion, and said lightly: "Remember, Mr Bester, you are TGB now. You don't have to eat at all. It won't hurt you. You won't even get hungry." He smiled dismissively and moved away soundlessly; he was there one moment and gone the next, as if he'd been switched off.

Reality washed over Fats like a curling wave. He felt that he was lying there drenched. He was TGB. He didn't have to eat. He couldn't eat—not the way he had before.

It takes a little training to get back into the habit, Carl had explained. Fats had never really got this. How could you get out of the habit? Now he observed that he had not felt hungry, or thirsty, since he had come out of the OR. He had put this down to trauma. Yet it was not stress suppressing his appetite, but rather that his appetite had been removed along with his stomach and all the rest of it. There was nothing left to feel hungry. He had read somewhere that some patients retained the sensation of hunger pangs, via pathways triggered in the brain, but he did not seem to be one of those.

Hunger was gone. An arc of anxiety surged through him: what would happen to his vital relationship with donuts now? Would he no longer desire them? Had he gone through this awful alteration in the name of saving his life, only to have the most important thing in his life become empty?

Fats endured eight days of mental agony in his hospital bed until he could send Carl out for donuts. So much for his blissfully pain-free recovery. He tried to face up to the specter of his fear: he would see, or smell, a donut and be unmoved. It would mean nothing to him: not pleasure, indulgence—can it be an indulgence if it's not bad for you?—or security. He would eat one of his own donuts, so utterly superior, and find it unsatisfying because it no longer answered any primal need. What had he done? Why had be yielded to the beguilings of that automaton Carl? This was a disaster. He would have to close his beloved shop and go and work for Carl as a waiter at NoFood, that palace of spiraling emptiness where those who did not need to eat were served by a chef who refused to cook. He was positively trembling with nerves when Carl showed up at his bedside with a crinkly bag. Fats snatched it out of his hands and unveiled two old-fashioned donuts. As soon as he saw them, and smelled them, and held the crumpled and greasy bag in his shaky fingers, he knew he would be alright. A tear or two leaked out from under his thankful eyelids.

Carl watched him from the bedside chair. "They're not Crystalline Donuts, of course," he said soothingly, "but they were the best I could do. This is not a donut neighborhood." To Fats the two donuts looked absolutely wonderful. He clasped them to his chest like life preservers. After a while he ate them slowly, one after the other, in a meditative ritual, just like Carl sitting in the shop at the front table in the sunlight.

Cena

"Can't Eat Normally Anyway?" said Donovan pointedly as she strode into the room in which Seychelles was seated next to her husband's body, just finishing her dinner. Her friend looked up and smiled weakly. Hardwicke Arar, the world-famous chef, had died six weeks ago, and Donovan had not been inside the house since. The motto of Floating Island had never seemed more eerily appropriate.

In the way of mottos, it had begun as a joke: Hardy had been looking down at his hands braiding together watercress stems as he stood in her gleaming kitchen at the inaugural dinner, surveying the array of pampered dishes that surrounded him, when he suddenly shrugged and said, "Well, seeing as you can't eat normally anyway..."

Donovan had laughed. It had been so typical of Hardy, so defiant, so splendidly wrongheaded in his conviction that the disgusting processes of organic digestion with which humans were born were preferable to the advanced technology that graced the insides of his elite TGB clientele. "That's us, Hardy," she had said, "Can't Eat Normally Anyway. C-E-N-A? *Cena*! Hah!"

"Lawyers' humor, I presume," said Hardy distantly. He hated to be caught unawares.

"Yeah. *Cena*—dinner. Meal. Feast. Latin. Just what we'll be having now, those of us who can't eat normally."

Hardy had let this pass. He was preoccupied; the success of the whole venture hung on this first evening, on Donovan

69

and her ten guests, culled from the anxious group of the three hundred and twenty-nine people stranded on his waiting list when he had closed the restaurant. Most of them were also her clients. These lucky few had been invited to attend the premiere evening of Arar's extraordinary new moveable feast.

Floating Island was a dining club—hardly unheard of—but extraordinary in the reversal it embodied: Hardwicke Arar, inventor of NoFood, his hands unsullied by meat and vegetables for almost twenty years, would come to your house and cook real food. Hardy was now in possession of two decades' worth of rarified menus, devised free of encumbering distractions, and he could now rely on a client base to whom no harm could be done by even the most radical experiments in cuisine, short of quick-acting poison.

So, either this moment marked the descent of the great chef of the imagination into the mundane, or the natural evolution of the NoFood concept. Hardy was in a fever, and Donovan was not surprised that he had no patience with her joke.

Still, the acronym hung on. "When's the next cena?" Seychelles would ask, poring over her calendars and lists of suppliers. "Maybe the fifteenth?"

"Fine," Hardy would say, absently. He let her take care of bookings. But Donovan was secretly proud to have her utterance enshrined, especially as it turned Hardy's words on their heads, deservedly.

Not, of course, that he had noticed.

Donovan looked down at Seychelles daintily wiping her lips with a white napkin as she sat beside her embalmed husband. She focused briefly on her friend's plate. "Veal, huh? Mushroom sauce?" Seychelles had a weakness for mushrooms. Most were now listed. Those worth having were, anyway, because of the whole wild mycelium deal; scientists still had them staked out everywhere, yakking on about network theory, totally missing the fact that mushrooms are for eating. It was irritating.

Seychelles had not called her to ask if there were any exceptions to the wild mushroom ban; normally she was a stickler for compliance. Maybe she was loosening up a bit in her time of grief; maybe the compliance had been Hardy's thing. It was certainly his style. Uptight.

Seychelles intercepted Donovan's glance at her plate. She knew exactly what was passing in her mind. "Well," she said defensively, "I'm not running a restaurant, am I?"

"Nope," replied Donovan. This made sense to her: Seychelles would not serve illegal food to her clients, but she might eat it herself. It was a matter of private conscience. This was an enabling distinction in embargo. Still, Donovan found that she was not comfortable invoking this idea in defense of Seychelles, with whom she had spent fruitless hours arguing over the propriety of listing. Like most people, Seychelles paid little attention to the government. Her determination to keep up with the ever-changing list of products under embargo—at least food products—was her one commitment. Donovan scoffed at it.

Yet now she felt, creepily, that disorder was spreading in the universe. Seychelles was eating listed mushrooms. She would never have done it while Hardy was alive.

Can't Eat Normally Anyway. Anymore?

Silenced by mushrooms, Donovan waited for Seychelles to get up. Hardy lay in his bed equally silent. She had to admit he was striking. He had always been striking, with that unfixed nose and a belly full of his own guts. She assumed they were not there now. Joined the rest of us a little late, didn't you, Hardy? Maybe if you'd had them out before, you wouldn't be dead. She had never asked Seychelles what he had died of. She didn't want Seychelles to have to explain. Hardy, you jerk. Why didn't you take better care of yourself? What's going to become of Floating Island now?

The crow's feet around the chef's eyes were smoothed out: he had finally discovered the cure for ageing. He was the only person she had ever known who had not been looking for it. It was wrong on him.

Seychelles stood up. She gazed at Hardy without speaking. She did not touch him. "Would you like tea?" she asked abruptly, turning away. "No? Then let's go. Did you come to discuss the business?" She picked up her plate and headed out the door toward the kitchen.

"I came to see you, but yes, also to discuss the business. I was wondering—might as well say it—if you wanted a new partner?"

"Who?"

"Me."

"But who would cook?"

"We would."

"Us?" asked Seychelles uncertainly. Hardy had been the best cook who ever lived. Donovan did not doubt it. Floating Island would be a different, lesser operation without him, but it was still marketable.

Donovan could not picture her life without it. If she had to step in to keep it going, fine. She was almost prepared to admit this to Seychelles. Floating Island was dear to her: most of its members were her friends; she got to see the insides of their houses and cook in their kitchens, which was strangely intimate. There was something wonderfully forbidden and secret about it, meeting up in these domestic sanctums to consume the food of Hardwicke Arar, dreamed of by thousands: NoFood made real. Come on.

It had also contributed substantially to her legal practice.

"We still have Hardy's menus. Or you do. You've cooked a lot of them yourself. Even I helped a lot of the time. We can't kill anyone. Think of it as a tribute to Hardy."

Seychelles could think of it in any way she chose. For Donovan, it would be a means of keeping together their small group, the elite within the elite who knew how to enjoy the true gift of total gastric bypass. She had been annoyed at how long it had taken the NoFood idea to die—it still prevailed in many places, though none that mattered—and had been secretly elated when Hardy had stepped back from it. All the peanut butter sandwiches she had eaten on the sly were suddenly validated. Real food was okay: the fashionable were no longer distracted by phastasms and could put their expensive interiors to good use. The thought of all those miles of empty high-grade tubing had always been offensive to her. She hated waste.

Seychelles looked thoughtful. "I thought I would just close up shop," she said, "I couldn't face going on after…" Her face blanked, then flushed slightly as she blurted out: "No. It's that I can't cook…I can't eat…without him! Remember how I couldn't eat at your place?" Donovan nodded. Seychelles had visited her for a few days right after her husband had died. "I can only do it at home. With him. And I can't risk losing it, Donovan—eating, eating Hardy's food, it's my last link to him, I—" Seychelles was looking shaky.

"Where's your puffer? Is it on the bureau? Do you want me to get it?"

"No, no! I'll be fine. Just give me a minute. It's so weird saying this. It's crazy. I need Hardy to be with me—in the house. Just looking at him for a while makes me hungry, and then I can cook. I come back and eat my meals with him. It's the only way I can do it. That's why I had him…preserved."

"You get hungry?" asked Donovan curiously. "How can you?"

"I don't know. It's some psychological effect. I always have; ever since I met him."

"I thought that was impossible."

"No, it's not. Rare, but not impossible."

"What does it feel like?" The hunger of her childhood had faded beyond recall.

"I don't know. Like pain. Itching. Anxiety. Hope. Wanting something. Wishing for someone to return who's away. It's hard to explain." She shook her head. "It can be dull and spreading, or sharp. It makes you feel like you have to *do* something."

"It doesn't sound like much fun."

"No, but it's necessary for me. It's part of me. I borrowed it from Hardy; he had it, that natural hunger. It's the only natural thing about me." Her taut face suppressed a sob.

"You don't have to be hungry to eat, Seychelles," said Donovan gently.

"No?"

"No. Look at me. I have been eating steadily for the past twenty-five years, and I've never been hungry at all." Seychelles looked calmer. Donovan cleared her throat and went on in her briskest lawyer's voice: "Now, returning to the business plan. We can cook. We can present Hardy's inimitable food to our gilded membership—"

Seychelles interrupted her in panic. "No! Donovan, I won't be able to do it, I know it! I can't cook without Hardy!"

"Well," said Donovan with her best deadpan, "Maybe we could bring him with us."

"What?" exclaimed Seychelles in horror, "How could we…?"

Donovan regarded her expressionlessly and continued: "Hardwicke Arar, the celebrated chef, could continue to preside over the meals he has so brilliantly devised, the centerpiece of every occasion—"

"Donovan!"

"He was never much of a talker—"

Seychelles snorted. Her face relaxed. Donovan smiled with relief. She had had no suspicion of Seychelles' acute state of mind. Turning her hospital suite into a mausoleum had struck her as flamboyant, not like Seychelles, whom she had never known to be fond of display, but she had known nothing of this strange dependence. The thought floated across her mind: did she really want to begin a business partnership with someone who was insane?

But she was fond of Seychelles and desperate to save Floating Island. If it came to tolerating this weird kick and trying to wean her friend slowly off dining *à deux* with her husband's body, so be it. Lawyers are always running into odd stories, even in embargo: the things people wanted to import, the things that the government sought to list, still sometimes blew her mind.

"Do you want me to look after the contract?" she asked, businesslike. A contract gives no quarter to anybody's bizarre sentiments.

"Fine," said Seychelles. She seemed to be agreeing. It was wonderful: Donovan was now half of Floating Island. The drama of the world's most exclusive catering was hers. She excused herself as soon as she could to get it all down on paper. She was so pleased she did all the work for free. After all, she was now a proprietor of Floating Island, and there was some reason to fear the business was at risk.

She came back the next day, carefully avoiding mealtimes, for Seychelles to sign. They read it over punctiliously—it was all virtuously in order—and wrote their names down. Donovan Donovan. Seychelles Xenobarbus. "I used to hate my name," said Donovan, meditatively, staring at her own writing. "But it's kind of grown on me. If it's good once, why not twice?"

"I always liked it," said Seychelles. They sat companionably for some while, discussing suppliers. Donovan felt that this was not the time to press about relaxing the policy on compliance. Now that she was an owner, she suddenly felt the attraction of integrity. It was novel. She would have to learn to keep her lawyer hat and her restaurateur hat on separate pegs. The idea was curiously satisfying. Whole new areas of temptation were opening up before her, on the other hand, now that she could buy wholesale. Not to mention the new leverage she would have at Bernini and Fiasco's for all those items she had on backorder. The sea urchins, especially. She had been waiting for those for three years.

She racked her mind for any of Hardy's recipes that might have involved sea urchin. Well, soon enough she could check for herself. Hardy and Seychelles had always been amazingly gracious about sharing their recipes with the members of Floating Island. Each one was probably worth thousands. Donovan had many already written down, those they had given her or those she had re-created from watching the cena preparations. It was one of the most valuable privileges of membership. But now she would have access to the whole file: every recipe created at NoFood, and those elaborated since. It was a goldmine.

"Oh yes," said Seychelles, when she asked about recent recipes: "There are quite a few new ones from the Island years. A hundred or so. Plus a few made-to-order, though you know he hated to do that. Only did it as a favor—or a joke, sometimes. Remember that birthday of yours?"

"With the fancy wine? The most mediocre meal ever cooked by Hardwicke Arar? That really put me in my place," said Donovan reminiscently. She had been enraged at the time, though. Her father had recently died, and she was recovering from some bad surgery, sufficiently bad that not even looking forward to the lawsuit was helping her along, when Hardy and Seychelles had appeared at her door. They wanted to create a particular dish, and thought that she would be able to help them out, having just inherited her father's unsurpassed wine cellar. She had been thrilled. She hit the access code for the cellar and let them find it: there was a map.

Then Hardy had gone to her kitchen and cooked a fussy rice dish with this fish and that sausage and the wine that was worth $70,000, and it had been deadly boring. She had been shocked. They all sat together and ate it, Donovan growing more and more incredulous, until Seychelles had pulled out of her bag a piece of pressed cotton paper on which was written, in the unforgettable cursive of the old headwaiter at NoFood, the utterly pretentious order she had made at the restaurant on the evening Seychelles was eighteen, when they had been given *carte blanche*. She had laughed and passed it off at the time and fumed about it after.

Yet their attention had been flattering: the famous chef had come to her house and cooked a meal for her, which had never happened before to anyone she had heard of. She had still stood quite in awe of Hardwicke Arar then. So even though she was angry, it had been invigorating. She had gotten a lot better after that. She also found, in retrospect, that she was pleased that the wine was lousy. Her father had been such a controlling bastard that it was a relief to find that at least one of the things he had stocked up on and stored away was not worth it. How much of all of this Seychelles had suspected, Donovan could not say, but in her present state of comradeship and euphoria she was willing to attribute a lot to her insight.

"They're all handwritten," continued Seychelles. "Mostly by him, but a few by Carl, and some by me. They're in a se-ries of books, just loose pages in pockets—I tried to get him to archive them, but he never would—filed by year. He had almost total recall of them, but it's a maddening system for anybody else."

"Whatever happened to Carl, anyway?"

"He died last year. He was a hundred and thirty."

"Not bad."

"He looked about twenty-two to the end. He was a won-derful waiter. He told me once he studied hypnosis. I always wondered about it. The most obnoxious people were cowed by him."

"I found him terrifying myself."

"He was a lovely man, really. That quietness in him went all the way to the bone."

"If they were his own bones. He must have had quite a surgery budget."

"Yes, he was addicted to surgery. Hardy always thought it was odd."

"Hardy thought all surgery was odd. He was odd."

"True." They discussed the ins and outs of reorganizing the recipes, which Seychelles had always been tempted to do. But Hardy had been adamant. "I'll find them," he had always insisted, "I know how they evolve." And he always had. Sey-chelles and Donovan, after some hesitation, decided to copy the recipes over to a searchable format but keep the original files as they were.

Seychelles was about to order a secretary to start the proj-ect when Donovan exclaimed, "Wait! Are you crazy? I'll do it! Copy the recipes of Hardwicke Arar, are you kidding? You can't let anyone else do it! Think what they're worth—to the business, to you! No way!" Seychelles wondered how she would find the time. "I'll find it! Don't worry about it. I can do it bit by bit, and meanwhile we can go on with Hardy's system."

They went on with Hardy's system. Donovan started out gamely on her scanning and transcribing but always found herself randomly reading, sifting through the pages. She worked slower, slower, and slower. Finally she gave up altogether.

So each cena they prepared began with the same leisurely shuffle. Their pre-banquet conferences grew longer and longer, often taking days. Strangely, they never quarreled about it. They argued about every other aspect of the business at one point or another. Yet when it came to choosing the recipes they would make, they inevitably reached a silent consensus that required only a little adjustment.

They didn't even really work together on it. Once a date was set, Donovan and Seychelles would each spend blocks of time in the library—they had taken to calling it "the library," though it was just a small annex with a single shelf and a desk—and then somehow meet up in the kitchen at the right time to say "I was looking at those veal sausages with apricot" or "Possibly that leek soup from the year—?" A menu would assemble itself.

Donovan could never quite get hold of what happened during this process. She would head into the library thinking she was looking for one thing that she particularly remembered or desired, look for it for a while—sometimes she even found it—and then fall into a kind of trance, glancing over this bit of paper and that bit of paper and their flat or crumpled edges. Hardy's bold black longhand, sometimes quite hard to read, Carl's elegant calligraphy, Seychelles' intense backward-slant printing, exerted a weird force: single lines or words would catch her attention for no reason and hang in front of her eyes; thoughts that had nothing to do with food would run through her mind. She would wander out of the room again surprised at how much time had passed and with no clear idea of her own conclusions. Then meeting Seychelles in the kitchen she would suddenly say "what about the—?" and find that they had both been thinking along the same lines. She was fairly sure that Seychelles imagined herself to be communing with Hardy on these occasions, but as for herself, she was not sure what went on. It was great business practice, though.

Floating Island went from strength to strength under their direction. It seemed the membership—forty-five in all—were as desperate to keep it going as Donovan had been. Everyone was really invested in it, even after the death of Arar. Indeed he became more talismanic; they began each meal with a solemn toast to him, as to an absent deity. Donovan felt that many people were secretly relieved; he had been an awkward personality in real life. Having someone of that magnitude in your kitchen or at your table could put you off your food.

Seychelles was still mourning. She did not eat at the dinners they made, though she had no problem cooking them. Donovan did not harass her about it. It was not like she actually *needed* to eat.

Donovan's mind would return every now and again to the sea urchins languishing on order at Fiasco's; she even went into the library once or twice with the intention of looking for a recipe. Yet somehow she never found one, always hearing Hardy's implacable voice in her head, urging her to cook something else, something legal, tasteful, courageous.

They had just finished their twenty-seventh cena, at the house of one of her colleagues in embargo that was a positive nest of confiscatable items, when she received a late-night call from Seychelles. "Donovan?" her friend whispered as if from the bottom of a mine shaft, "I just got a call from the company that did Hardy's embalming. They asked me for permission to transfer the remains they have in their vault; they're moving. Apparently they have to do that if there might be any live tissue in the sample."

"In the sample?" asked Donovan stupidly, trying not to yawn.

"I didn't even know they stored anything. It's policy, apparently. You know people are so maniacal about saving everything. Well, they have everything they took from Hardy, including a semen sample." Her voice cut out, then returned. "Do you hear me, Donovan?"

Donovan heard her.

Her heart was suddenly wrung for Seychelles, for the last dilemma in which Hardy had placed her. One of his list of weird aversions had been to VF; he had freaked out completely when Seychelles had tried to go ahead normally with fertilization and surrogacy early in their marriage. He had run off and nearly gotten himself killed in the Asias. What would she do now, faced with this chance and the memory of Hardy's disapproval, when his specter still haunted her most trivial choices, like compliance? She heard Seychelles heaving on her puffer at the other end.

"Should I come over?"

"No," Seychelles gasped, "I think I'll be fine. I'm completely tranked anyway. But I wanted to ask you if you'd come with me to pick up the sample tomorrow. I'm going to see if it's viable."

Donovan was quiet.

"I have to know, Donovan."

"Of course you do. I'll come with you."

"Thank you," said Seychelles.

The sample was viable. It took three days to determine this; it was in a delicate condition. For three days Seychelles talked clinically about "the sample" as if thereby she could divorce it from the body and memory of Hardy. She did not eat and shunned his room. Donovan stayed with her. She was sitting with her in the living room when the news came. She was frankly desperate for something to eat, just to relieve the tedium—she was even beginning to wonder if she might be hungry—but it seemed an inauspicious time to cook. She sat where she was, trying not to drum her fingers on her leg.

"Right," said Seychelles, standing up as soon as she was off the phone. "I'm going to the hospital to set up the surrogacy. Call the insurers for me, will you, so they can send over the paperwork?"

Donovan was stunned. Where was the woman who so carefully hoarded up her husband's recipes like divine directives? She caught a vanishing glimpse of Seychelles' swinging hair as she swept out the front door.

Eight months later, Hardy and Seychelles' daughter was born. Seychelles named her Cena. Donovan immediately dropped her use of the term at Floating Island. It seemed disrespectful. After all, she was the baby's second legal parent.

Seychelles had first asked her to do this in her capacity as her lawyer, and she had agreed. It was a formality, though a flattering one; Seychelles had plenty of lawyers. She had not seen too much of her over the gestation period, however. Seychelles had taken the unusual step of inviting the surrogate into her house for the duration, giving her a room in the hospital suite. Not Hardy's room, which she kept locked. The surrogate, whose name was Ananda, saw her carrying food in there every evening and naively wondered if she kept her own shrine.

Donovan had found she could not be in the same room as Ananda for long, especially after she was visibly pregnant. She had never seen a pregnant woman before; every female she knew was TGB. All their ovaries were on ice, and their uteruses who knew where. Incinerated?

She could not take Ananda: it was like looking at a sheep. She avoided the house as long as she was there except for minimal business purposes. Once the child was delivered, though, she found herself there constantly. Despite the fact that she had a live-in pediatrician and a nursing staff of three, Seychelles was always calling her in the middle of the night, or at the dangerous period around six a.m., whenever the baby was restless, sick, sleepless, or exceptionally cute.

Donovan took an extended leave of absence from her practice—her interest in embargo had been flagging, anyway, except as it affected their choices at Floating Island—and moved over to Seychelles' place. It was vast and well-staffed, so there was no problem. It was much easier to get out of bed when Seychelles buzzed her on the intercom and run down the hall than to drag herself wearily out to the helipad yet again for a journey across town. So she said in longsuffering tones to the rest of the members of Floating Island from time to time. Quite often, in fact. It became a common refrain: the law never sleeps.

Donovan did not run down the hall to please her client Seychelles. She ran down the hall to placate Cena, and feed her, and burp her, and clothe her, and calm her: Cena loved Donovan. The baby was a yelling ball of viscera; she threw up on her regularly: Cena loved Donovan.

Hardy was still reposing in his room. Cena had seen him—she crawled everywhere, and had an early facility with doors—but without registering any meaning. In her first week of walking, after she had staggered seven steps and collapsed triumphantly in Donovan's arms, she gestured insistently toward the hospital wing and tried to get Donovan to take her to see "doy-ee, doy-ee?" Dolly. Donovan experienced a chill.

She spent two days struggling with tactful formulas to express her fears of what living with her embalmed father might do to a toddler's psyche when Seychelles came to another one of her moments of decision.

"I've called the company again," she announced one day as she oversaw Cena's breakfast in her highchair, "and they are bringing the rest of Hardy's remains out of storage. They'll be here tomorrow."

"Here?" asked Donovan, confounded.

"Yes," said Seychelles, brightly. "I've asked them to put it all back in, everything they took out. They were a bit surprised."

"I bet," said Donovan.

"It's the right thing for Hardy. He should be fully himself, not all stuffed with junk. Then we can have his funeral."

"Good," said Donovan.

Two days later Hardwicke Arar was in the ground. It was quiet for a celebrity funeral, just Seychelles and Donovan and Cena, but then most people had given up hoping for it. They did not invite the members of Floating Island, as they felt the moment had passed for anyone but family.

Donovan watched the biodegradable casket descend slowly into the black. Seychelles stepped forward alone for a minute before they closed the casket and touched Hardy's face. She said something to him, but Donovan did not hear what it was. She came back and took Cena from Donovan so she could hold her while the winch did its job. "It's the first time I ever spoke to him," she said to Donovan conversationally, "Since he died." Donovan waited for more. "It was never about talking with us."

"No," agreed Donovan solemnly. "It was about eating."

"Eating! Yes. Eating."

They watched Cena chew on her scarf.

Author Biography

Sarah Tolmie trained as a medievalist at the University of Toronto and Cambridge and is on faculty in the English Department at the University of Waterloo. She has been fascinated by the weird fourteenth-century visionary poem *Piers Plowman*, which inspired her novel *The Stone Boatmen*, for the past decade. NoFood is likewise based in part on one scene in the poem known as the Feast of Conscience. She is a longtime poet and recently published the chapbook *Sonnet in a Blue Dress and Other Poems* with Baseline Press, which will be followed by a 120-sonnet collection, *Trio*, with McGill-Queen's University Press in April 2015.

Its strangeness fascinates, captivates.
∞Ursula K. Le Guin

...a powerfully original first novel.... At any moment,
beauty may strike with random grace, and unpretentious
little details evoke the sense of wonder.

~Faren Miller, *Locus*

In Tolmie's novel, writing becomes a holy act, temple
birds carry an ancient grief, and statues that never move
are eerily alive. You will want to find such places once
you've finished reading this remarkable novel.

~Nancy Hightower, *The Washington Post*

I cannot recall reading anything quite like it in recent
years. It is perhaps a little early in the reading year to say
this but I am sure already that it will be one of my books
of 2014.

~Maureen Kincaid Speller, *Strange Horizons*